PISTOLERO

A BEATRIX ROSE THRILLER

MARK DAWSON

1

The jungle is merciless to old men.

Father Jair Beltrano had been walking for three hours. His two guides travelled lightly through the forest in sandals, making no more sound than the breeze, while Father Beltrano crashed along behind, breaking branches, slipping in mud pools and grunting painfully as his old knees grated like jagged glass.

All of this Father Beltrano could have borne if it hadn't been for the sheer relentlessness of the heat. He was used to the stifling dampness of the town, but up here on the forested slopes, the heat took on a new dimension; it made his clothes stick to his skin like wet wadding and the sweat run into his eyes. Clouds of black flies rose from every mud pool and swarmed about him like smoke, lancing the bare skin on his face and arms until the flesh swelled into puffy red boils.

He paused to sit on the twisted roots of a kapok tree.

"How much farther?" he gasped.

It was the third time he had asked in the past half hour.

His two guides, as always, were the model of patience.

"Another hour, Father," said Diego. "Two at the most. We must take the long way around the mountain to avoid being seen. But don't worry; we will be back before dark."

His companion, Ezra, was the quieter of the two men and spoke no English. While Diego talked, Ezra watched, looking around and listening to things Father Beltrano could only imagine. Now he spoke rapidly to Diego in Arecuna.

"He says we should go now," said Diego when Ezra finished, turning back to the priest. "He says we are not alone on this mountain."

Without further explanation, the two guides turned and set off again. Father Beltrano breathed a heavy sigh. Ever since their trip had begun, his guides had been nervous about imagined noises and phantom pursuers. Father Beltrano was beginning to think it was an act they were putting on for his benefit, possibly in the hopes of a better tip at the end of the journey.

He pulled himself painfully to his feet and stumbled over one of the twisted roots. He fell, face first, hitting the ground with a crash that split his chin on a stone. His two companions were back in an instant, helping him to his feet.

"Are you all right, Father?" enquired Diego. "Are you hurt?"

Father Beltrano released himself from Diego's grasp and wiped the blood from his chin, angry with himself now. "I'm all right. I'm fine. Don't fuss over me."

A terrible thought struck him, and he tore open the flap of the leather satchel around his shoulders. Nestling inside, wrapped in a cloth, was a small glass bottle filled with dirty brown liquid. Father Beltrano sighed with relief. To have come all this way and lost the sample at this stage would have been more than his old bones could have stood right now.

He forced himself to slow his breathing. "I'm all right," he said again, more to reassure himself than the others. "Everything's all right. We can go on now."

His companions did not answer. Father Beltrano saw they had both adopted the same still pose, looking into the middle distance with noses raised, like dogs, sampling the air. "What is it now?" He couldn't quite keep the irritation from his voice.

Diego raised a hand for silence. The old priest listened, but all he could hear was the whine of a billion insects intent on consuming his flesh. Saints preserve him, this was too much. At this rate they would not be home until hours after dark.

"Enough of this," he said, more gruffly than he intended. "Nothing moves out there except for the good Lord, and he is on our side. Now come on. We must go."

Diego started to protest. "Please, Father, wait," he hissed. "We have to—"

He did not complete his sentence. He grunted, and his head snapped backwards, his legs folding beneath him as he collapsed into the leaf litter. For a moment, Father Beltrano stared in shock at his guide, watching the arterial spray that misted from the gaping wound in the man's skull. Then he cried out in alarm, staggering backwards against the tree.

A second slug splintered the trunk inches from Father Beltrano's head. His breath came hot and fast, and he felt the panic rising in his chest. Then Ezra was beside him, pulling at his sleeve and speaking in broken English.

"Father, Father—come now. Come now!"

Father Beltrano allowed Ezra to drag him away from the clearing, leaving the fallen Diego behind. Ezra pulled him into the cover of the trees and began to urge him up the steep slope beyond. "To the mountain. To the mountain," he hissed urgently.

Father Beltrano scrambled upwards through the thick undergrowth, gasping for breath; his chest burned, and his legs screamed for mercy. Another shot split the leaves above their heads. He could hear an engine now, the diesel roar of a heavy pickup, and the sounds of whooping and hollering.

Father Beltrano slithered and fell on the slimy rocks. He continued the climb on hands and knees as Ezra coaxed him forward.

The noise of the truck receded as they moved up the slope, and now Father Beltrano could hear a faint thundering that seemed to come from above them. Pain gripped the old priest's chest, and his throat tasted raw and metallic. "Please..." he gasped. "I have to... stop..."

"Near there, Father. Near there."

Somehow, Ezra managed to drag Father Beltrano up the last few metres of the slope to a point where the foliage thinned and the ground levelled out. The old man sank to his knees and instinctively clutched at the silver cross that hung at his neck, muttering a desperate prayer in Latin.

Ezra had brought him to a flat stretch of rocky ground. Metres away, a mountain river surged from the forest and ran swiftly across the plateau before plunging over a vertical drop into the jungle canopy below. A thick column of mist rose above the cliff edge.

Father Beltrano looked desperately to Ezra. "Where next?" he yelled above the roar of the waterfall.

Ezra pointed emphatically across the fast-flowing water

to the trees on the other side, emphasising the direction with several thrusts of his muscular brown hand. "Father go," he cried above the rushing water. "You go. Ezra stay."

Before Father Beltrano could stop him, the small Indian had gathered up his rifle and turned back down the slope, scrambling away into the foliage. Father Beltrano cried out, but the man had already gone.

He was alone.

He looked back at the river. It looked treacherous, the fast-flowing current tumbling over a jagged bed of slippery green rocks. One misstep would put him in the water and carry him over the edge in a heartbeat. But if he did not leave, he would have to face what was behind him. The priest knew well enough who they were, and he had seen what they did to anyone caught on the mountain.

It was no choice at all.

He scrambled to his feet and staggered forward, clutching the precious satchel to his chest. At the water's edge, however, he hesitated, his resolve wavering.

The river was a beast, fully charged by its rush down the mountain. It looked capable of knocking him off his feet in an instant. He took a tentative step into the shallow waters at the edge.

The roar of a diesel engine came from behind him, and a Land Cruiser burst out of the forest. The men standing in the back pointed at him excitedly and banged on the roof of the vehicle. To his horror, Father Beltrano watched the truck turn and bounce towards him, stopping a dozen metres away.

The two men in the back jumped down. Both were Indians like his guides, but wearing expressions of casual cruelty. They kept their weapons levelled on him.

Two more men climbed from the main cabin. They were

white; one was muscular and bearded, his companion smaller and wiry.

"Give it up, Padre," the smaller man called. His voice was accented. Australian, thought the priest, or maybe South African. "Give us the satchel. We know what you've got in there. Give it up now, and we all get to go home."

The larger man walked up to Father Beltrano and held out his hand. The priest instinctively clutched the bag tighter.

"They're dying," Father Beltrano said. "The people. The children. You know what's happening here, yet you do nothing."

His companion hawked noisily and spat as he stepped up beside the taller man. "We all got our jobs to do, Padre. This one's mine." Definitely Australian.

He glanced at the big man and gave him a nod, and the man lunged forward and grabbed the bag from Father Beltrano. The priest made a brief show of resisting, but the big man punched him hard in the face, breaking his glasses. Father Beltrano fell back into the shallows.

The Australian laughed. "Hurts like a bitch, don't it? I had mine busted a few times."

There was a loud pop from across the clearing, and the big man suddenly collapsed to one knee, clutching at the flesh of his calf.

"Jesus Christ on a fucking bicycle," he yelled. "I'm fucking hit!"

The Australian snapped to attention, scanning the edge of the clearing until he found what he was looking for. "There," he cried. "On our six. By the trees."

With horror, Father Beltrano saw Ezra standing at the edge of the forest with his rifle in his hands. He was struggling with the ancient bolt action, trying to engage the next round in the chamber; he never completed the task. Automatic fire from four weapons cut through his body and sent him backwards into the undergrowth.

The Australian spat again. "Jungle vermin. You leave them alone for five minutes and the fuckers spring up everywhere."

Father Beltrano took advantage of the distraction. He got to his feet and waded out into the river.

"Watch it," the Australian yelled. "The fucking padre's getting away."

The icy water bit through Father Beltrano's clothes and made him gasp. His feet slithered and slipped on the green rocks, and once he stumbled and went right under, but he forced himself to his feet again and shoved himself onwards. He had to get to the other side. He had to tell what he had seen. The lives of others depended on it.

He was ten metres out from the shore when he heard the shout.

"Padre—get the fuck back here."

The old priest stopped and turned slowly in the middle of the river. The Australian's rifle was pointed directly at the priest's chest. Father Beltrano instinctively clutched at the cross around his neck, taking comfort and courage from its familiar feel.

"You will not kill me," he shouted confidently. "I have the protection of the Lord Jesus Christ. He has tasked me with telling the world about your crimes, and you cannot stop me. With His protection, I cannot die."

The Australian grinned. "I wouldn't be so sure," he said, and pulled the trigger.

Father Beltrano felt the punch in his chest before he

heard the crack of the bullet. A white-hot pain spread through his ribs and down both arms as the breath was forced from his lungs. He fell to his knees for the last time, as though in prayer, and then sank slowly beneath the surface of the water.

2

The agent on the check-in desk wore a patient smile.

"I'm *terribly* sorry," she said, sounding like she wasn't sorry at all. "But I'm afraid your connecting flight to Santiago has been cancelled."

Beatrix Rose sighed. "Why?"

"Technical issues." Her smile had all the warmth of an interior fridge light.

"When's the next one?"

The woman looked down at her screen. "Not until tomorrow morning. There's one seat left in economy."

"That'll do," she said.

After several minutes of exchanging passports, credit cards and boarding passes, Beatrix walked away and contemplated an eleven-hour wait in the barren retail wasteland of Venezuela's Tomás de Heres Airport. If she ever made it back to civilisation, she would make sure that Michael Yeung only ever booked her connecting flights through major airport hubs. Preferably in countries with a functioning economy.

Her options tonight were limited to a few chain restaurants, coffee shops, and a souvenir shop selling religious icons and fake Panama hats. She had her iPad, a crappy airport thriller and a solitary cannabis-infused cigarillo she had picked up in Trinidad on her last job for Michael.

That job had been simple enough. She had been sent to persuade a local freight manager in Port of Spain that his best interests lay in not skimming any more of the cargo his triad customers had entrusted to him. She had barely got beyond breaking the man's nose before he had begged for mercy and returned all of the goods he had stolen from previous shipments. It had been a job that was barely worthy of her, but one she had done willingly.

What she was interested in was the payoff. Michael owed her, and there was something she wanted in return.

Something she wanted *very* badly.

She took a hard plastic seat in a quiet section of the departure hall, with her back to a wall and a clear view of the exits. The airport was almost empty at this time of night. An elderly couple sat near to their departure gate, clutching their bags on their laps so that they would be ready when their flight was called. A backpacker lay stretched out on a row of seats, and a young businesswoman typed urgently into a laptop balanced on her knees.

Beatrix sighed. With so much time to kill, she could easily make it into the city, take a look around, have a nice meal.

Get stoned.

She smothered the thought. Best to keep focused. She was here on company business, and who knew what enemies Michael had in this part of the world. Besides, she had better things to think about. She closed her eyes and let the background hum of conversation and PA announcements wash over her as she tried to focus on what came next.

Four days ago, Michael had given her the news that he had located her daughter, Isabella. She was living, he said, with an adopted family in New Zealand after Control had placed the child there to give himself leverage over her. Michael said he understood how important it was for Beatrix to find her, and that was why he had invested his own money to track her down. It was also why he would pay Beatrix's expenses to go there and find her.

Just as soon as she had completed the job in Trinidad.

Part of her wondered if she was being played. Perhaps after Trinidad there would be another job, then another, and another. And each time, the prize of finding Isabella would be snatched away at the last moment, like a ball of wool yanked out of reach of a kitten.

She sighed. Paranoid thinking didn't help. Michael had promised her that as soon as she had finished in Trinidad, she should make her way to New Zealand. When she arrived there, he would send her the address where she could find Isabella. Michael might be many things, but he was not stupid. Pissing her off wouldn't be a good idea.

She opened her eyes as two policemen strode across the concourse towards her. She swore under her breath. Had she been too complacent? Had Control found her? She dismissed the thought. If this was Control, then he would have sent assassins, not cops. She would not have even seen them coming.

She smiled as they approached her seat.

"Helen Archer?"

"That's right. How can I help you?"

The shorter of the two men gestured towards a pair of doors marked *Sin Entrada*. "Would you come with us, please, Señora?"

"Why? What's this about?"

The policeman smiled. "You have an urgent call from Hong Kong. A friend of yours would like to talk to you."

Michael.

Her hopes lifted. Perhaps he was calling to give her Isabella's address. Then they sank just as quickly. That was not the arrangement. And Michael never changed an arrangement. This was something else.

She got to her feet. "Fine. Lead the way."

The officers led her out through the double doors. Instead of taking her to an office, however, they led her out through another set of security doors and back into the main hall. She followed them across the arrivals area and then outside into the warmth of a humid evening. There was a black limousine double-parked in front of the taxi rank. One of the police officers gestured towards the car, then saluted smartly and walked away.

The passenger door on the limo swung open. She approached cautiously and climbed into the back.

The driver turned. "Good evening. The phone, please." He gestured to a handset in the armrest of her seat. She lifted it to her ear.

"What are you doing, Michael?"

"I am sorry, Beatrix," he said. "I needed to speak to you."

"I'm supposed to be on a flight to Santiago."

"There will be other flights. Something has come up. It is important."

Beatrix cursed under her breath. It looked like it was kitten-and-ball-of-wool time. "That wasn't our arrangement. I'm going to see Isabella."

"Plans have changed. I am sorry for the inconvenience." He was being overcourteous, which Beatrix knew was a danger sign. It was the closest Michael ever came to giving a warning.

She sat back in the seat, stifling a sigh of irritation. Isabella would have to wait a little longer.

The limo pulled away from the kerb.

"Where am I going?" she said into the handset.

"You have a suite booked for the night at the Posada Don Carlos," Michael said. "One of the nicest hotels in Ciudad Bolivar. Very comfortable."

"But I'm not going there to relax?"

"I am afraid not. A man named Aurelio Rincon will meet you. He is very important to us."

"How?"

"His business interests intersect with my own. And he has a problem that requires your attention."

Beatrix looked out of the window at Bolivar City's old-world colonial houses and long streets that gave glimpses of the broad brown ribbon of the Orinoco. Despite the late hour, traffic was heavy, liberally salted with two-stroke Japanese motorcycles that threaded through the slow-moving cars like angry hornets.

Michael was being coy, which was not like him. Something about this job was making him uneasy.

"I'm going to need more background than that," she prompted him.

There was a long pause. "Rincon has a number of interests that coincide with mine," he said eventually. "Shipping, manufacturing, mining. His shipping line provides us with a secure export route to South American markets."

Beatrix gave a humourless smile. So that was it. For the last eighteen months, Michael had invested heavily in the production of methamphetamine on an industrial scale, utilising the skills of a professor from the University of Hong Kong who had inadvisably accrued a lot of debt in one of Michael's gambling dens. As a result, Michael now had a lot of meth, too much for the local market. He would need logistical support to export it. It sounded as if Rincon had the infrastructure to move the product into lucrative markets in South America.

It was little wonder that Michael wanted this job treated as a priority.

"Tell me what you need me to do."

"Thank you, Beatrix. Rincon has a gold mine called El Corazon De Oro in the foothills of the Guiana Highlands. It's one of the most lucrative mines in Venezuela and provides the funding for the rest of his operations. But he has a domestic labour problem. A local rebel group has been giving him problems. Disrupting mining operations, attacking his workers. He needs the problem dealt with."

Beatrix frowned. "Surely he has his own people to do that sort of thing?"

"He says that's out of the question. It has to be someone from outside the country."

"He wants to keep his own hands clean in case someone starts pointing fingers."

"Almost certainly. Rincon has political enemies who would like to make capital from this sort of thing. He needs a professional with no connections to him."

"And here I am," she said. "A convenient coincidence. How long will it take?"

"I don't believe this will detain you for long. A few days at most."

"And what about Isabella?"

"She will still be waiting for you when you are done. The more quickly you resolve Rincon's problem, the sooner you can be with her."

3

The hotel was comfortable and well-appointed in the traditional style, with dark wood furniture and tiled floors. The building was set back from the street, which was buzzing with the Friday night crowds enjoying the warm air. Beatrix climbed out of the limousine, pulling her bag after her. The driver closed the door and handed her a small yellow envelope.

"Your key card," he said. "First floor."

Beatrix crossed the lobby and rode the elevator up. As soon as she opened the door to her room, she noticed two things: the 'room' was an understatement for the vast bridal suite that lay before her, and there was a man waiting for her.

"Good evening, Miss Archer."

He sat in an armchair in the living-room area, facing the door, with his legs crossed and his hands resting lightly on the arms. He wore a pale linen suit with a dark blue dress shirt, two buttons open at the neck. He was overweight, his stomach bulged against his shirtfront, and his silver-grey beard had been carefully trimmed to cover a double chin.

An unsubtle gold chain hung around his neck, gleaming softly in the low light of the room.

"Señor Rincon?"

He smiled and inclined his head in her direction. "Please —you must call me Aurelio. Michael has told me about you. I am very pleased to finally have the chance to meet."

Beatrix closed the door behind her and dropped her bag on the luggage rack beside it, but did not move farther into the room. She leaned against the wall and assessed Rincon carefully. He had an air of arrogance that she had seen before, usually in the faces of the triad chiefs who worked with Michael. It came from a combination of extreme wealth and an unwavering certainty that their needs trumped everyone else's. There was also a wolfish leer in his eyes that she had also seen before. She wondered if he thought he was buying more than just her martial skills. She didn't want to upset Michael, but if Rincon made any unwanted advances, she would break one of his fingers.

Rincon gestured to the bar. "Please, Señora... a drink, perhaps, before business?"

She nodded, then made her way across the thick carpet and took a seat on the sofa facing him. "Whisky and soda."

Rincon stood and made his way to the drinks cabinet. He had surprisingly small feet for a man of his bulk, and he stepped lightly, like a dancer. She took the heavy cut glass tumbler that he offered her.

"Whisky and soda for you," he said, "and an aguardiente for myself. You know this drink? Sugar cane and anise. It is the drink of the poor people of Colombia. I drink it to remind myself of my roots. It seems very sweet, but it will punish you if you underestimate its strength." He smiled again, widely enough to allow her to see his gold front tooth.

Beatrix took a slug of scotch and decided she'd had enough small talk. "Mr. Yeung tells me you have a problem."

He made a solemn face and nodded. "Indeed, I do. Did he tell you I am in the mining business? Nickel, copper, iron ore, bauxite and, of course, gold. My mines are profitable and well run. I am a major employer in this part of the country, and I always look after my people. They receive good wages, food, accommodation, medical care. They want for nothing, and they are grateful to me for all I do for them. I am a man of the people, Señora Archer."

"If you say so."

"I have always enjoyed peace and prosperity in my mines. But now I have a scorpion in my shoe. *Banditos.* A racketeer who goes by the name of Fuego de la Muerte."

Beatrix frowned. "Fire of Death? Very melodramatic."

"What do you expect? The man is a thief and a communist. He and his men live in the forests around Prosperidad, and they prey on my gold mine. They steal equipment, attack my guards and terrorise my workers. Last month they attacked the payroll office and got away with over one hundred and twenty million bolivars."

"Five hundred dollars?" Beatrix stared at him curiously. "Why don't you just call the police?"

Rincon let out a dry laugh. "Police? *Please.* Prosperidad is over a hundred and fifty miles from Bolivar City. If I reported Fuego's many crimes, it would be at least six months before they even came to take a statement. No, the police are no good to me. The law has no reach in that part of Venezuela."

Beatrix shrugged. "What about your own people? Surely you have security?"

Rincon nodded. "More than a dozen men. All ex-special forces and very reliable. But their responsibilities are many, and they cannot be everywhere at once. I need someone who can deal with this scum on his own terms. Find out where he lives in the forest and take him out for good—it's the only way to stop the attacks. You know what they say, Miss Archer—sever the head and the body will die."

Beatrix took a deep breath. A skirmish between Rincon's security and a local bandit sounded very much like something she did *not* want to get involved with.

"I'm not sure I can help you," she said as evenly as possible. "It sounds like you need someone with local knowledge. Someone who can track Fuego. He can't be living in the forest without support. Have you tried asking anyone in the town if they know where he can be found?"

Rincon's expression clouded over, and she saw that something dangerous lurked underneath. She had evidently touched a nerve.

"The locals cannot always be relied on," he said tightly. "One thing you will learn about Venezuelans, Miss Archer: you can give them everything they might possibly need and still they will stab you through the heart if they get the chance. There are those in Prosperidad who see Fuego as a hero. One man against the establishment. They have developed strange notions about how he is a freedom fighter and a man of the people, and some have even suggested he is the reincarnation of the great Simon Bolivar himself." He snorted and drained his glass. "You see what I am up against, Miss Archer? I cannot fight a myth. I need him dead, and I need you to do it in such a way that everyone gets the message. You do not fuck with me and live."

So that was it. This wasn't about a bandit or a rebel leader. This was about Rincon's ego, pure and simple. His pride had been stung.

Beatrix finished her drink and set it on the glass table by

her side. "I'm still not convinced this is something I can help you with."

Rincon clenched his jaw. "I was told by Michael that you were a professional. He assured me that—"

"I *am* a professional. But this isn't a part of the world I know. Michael knows this. You're asking me to tackle a group of armed men in a jungle where they have the benefit of familiarity and local support. Chances are I'd end up dead. And if they found out that you sent me, you'd be a laughing stock."

Rincon frowned. The threat to his reputation was clearly something that gave him pause for thought.

"No," he said. "I have a good security team, and I will put them at your disposal. They will be able to track him down. Your job will be to dispose of him. Please, Señora Archer, humour me. Come with me to Prosperidad for a few days. If you still don't think it is something you can help me with, then perhaps we can still part on good terms."

Beatrix sighed. There was an unspoken threat there: If you *don't* come with me, you will have made an enemy. Part of her wanted to turn Rincon down. She wanted to tell him that she wasn't a mercenary and that she didn't fight other people's wars. But Michael had thought this job was important enough to send her here and had made it clear that Rincon's business was important. Michael knew where Isabella was. She couldn't afford to annoy him.

"All right," she said. "I'll come. But I'm not promising this is something that I can help you with."

Rincon clapped his hands. "Excellent. I have some business in Bolivar first thing in the morning, and then I will pick you up. Shall we say at eleven? We will fly directly to my compound near the mine. I will introduce you to my men, and you can get started."

4

Beatrix waited at the front of the hotel, wearing a pair of mirrored aviator shades and smoking a Marlboro. She had spent a restless night in her room, pacing to and fro and turning over all the ways the job might go wrong. Her anxieties had reached the point where she had contemplated taking a cab into downtown Bolivar to see if she could score some opium. But she had dismissed that idea at once. She had not returned to her old habit since Michael had paid for her rehabilitation. It wasn't that she abstained out of any loyalty to him. But he was the only one who could tell her where to find Isabella, and she was not about to do anything that would give him reason to be upset with her; she wouldn't function properly if she was high.

The cravings had subsided this morning and left her with a bitch of a headache. The one thing she didn't need right now was a helicopter ride with Rincon. She was relieved, then, when the limousine pulled up in front of the hotel and he was not inside.

"Señor Rincon sends his apologies," said the driver. "He

has been detained on business. He will go straight to the airport and meet you there."

Beatrix said nothing. That suited her just fine. She climbed in, sank back in the seat and closed her eyes. The driver pulled away, and twenty minutes later they arrived at the airport. They drove onto the apron, coming to a stop beside an executive Bell 206 JetRanger helicopter.

Rincon was already inside. The rotors were already beginning to turn as she stepped up into the cabin and took the leather bucket seat next to him, putting on the headphones that he offered as the pilot throttled up.

"Did you sleep well, Miss Archer?"

"Well enough."

She turned and looked out of the window. The helicopter lifted into the air and turned towards the south. They swept over the industrial districts that had metastasised around the edges of the airport, which then quickly gave way to an unbroken carpet of green, softening the steep peaks and valleys of the foothills. The thick foliage was unbroken for most of the journey, save for the occasional tributary of sluggish brown water that cut curves across the forest floor. Here and there she saw colourful birds startled into the air by the helicopter. She saw smoke rising from cooking fires. She saw a collection of low buildings clustered along the banks of a river, with corrugated roofs and walls painted in vivid turquoises and blues. There were people in the forest, she realised, but they were well hidden and far from the beaten track.

Finding Fuego del Muerte was going to be difficult.

They had been in the air for fifty minutes when the helicopter banked sharply and began to descend towards a flat-topped mountain in the distance. Rincon pressed the talk button on his headset.

"To get here by road would take half a day." He gestured to the view through the window to her left. "You will have a good view of El Corazon De Oro as we come in to land. It's magnificent."

The mountain grew larger until it filled the view on one side of the helicopter. She could see the mine clearly now, gouged into the hillside like an open wound. Great steps had been hewn into the rock, each one wide enough for two dump trucks. Thick rivers of chocolate-brown slurry ran down the rockface and continued most of the way down the mountainside like a smear of filth against the velvety green foliage. As they drew closer, Beatrix was struck by the true vastness of the mine. It was as though an enormous lake had been drained to leave behind a muddy basin. She could see a network of slatted wooden ladders arranged to allow the workers access to the lower tiers of the pit. Gangs of workers laboured with cutting tools, while others ferried away baskets of freshly hewn ore or trained high-pressure hoses against the loose rock. The workers, like everything else, were slathered in mud.

Rincon was beaming. "You see that? *That* is the Venezuelan dream. Before I came here, this was nothing but a backwater. It took a man like me to tear the wealth out of this land with my bare hands. Now every worker you see down there produces ten thousand times the cost of their wages in a single day."

"What do they earn?"

Rincon waved a hand dismissively. "You'd have to ask my CFO. Enough. And this place gives them much more than just a wage. They have security, a place to live, medical care... They are grateful to be here." He pointed. "Look—there is Prosperidad."

At the base of the mountain a wide track led into a shantytown of rickety homes that were crammed together chaotically, like flotsam that had been washed there by a flood. Even from this height, Beatrix could see that the buildings were ramshackle affairs of sodden wood and cinderblock with corrugated tin roofs. The streets that ran between them were thick with mud. They teemed with people, with stray dogs and chickens dotting the spaces between. She saw barefoot children pointing up at the helicopter as though it was an object of wonder. It reminded Beatrix of the *favelas* in Brazil and the barrios in Angola. She had been to both: teeming hubs of poverty, sickness and desperation.

"Prosperidad is a company town?"

Rincon nodded. "For many, it is the first home they have had that didn't have a roof made of branches and leaves. Our employment package is generous."

Beatrix looked down again and doubted that Rincon's definition of generous would match her own.

The shacks thinned out as they neared the edge of town, and the jungle reasserted itself, making for a dense green perimeter around the town and the mine. As they circled around the side of the mountain, a walled compound swung into view. A twelve-foot steel fence surrounded it, a guard tower squatted on each corner, and she could see a gate with a guardhouse. Inside the compound, a wide strip of asphalt ran between two modern buildings that were built in the colonial style with big windows and wraparound decking. The larger of the two buildings was two storeys high and the size of an out-of-town supermarket, while the other was a bungalow, set a little apart from the main building in its own gardens. There were two swimming pools and several hot tubs. Beyond the large house, Beatrix could see tennis courts and a manicured lawn the size of a football pitch.

The helicopter swung low over the property. Beatrix

suspected the flight path had been arranged for her benefit, allowing her to take in all that Rincon had built here. They descended towards a black helipad down the hill on a small rise outside the main compound and touched down with a soft judder. The engines whined down to a standstill while the pilot cut the electrics and shut off the fuel.

Rincon had climbed out of the craft before the blades had stopped turning. Beatrix stepped out after him, ducking her head.

"Let's get out of this damned heat," he said. "I need to freshen up, and then we can have a drink and talk properly. I'm looking forward to showing you my little empire."

A pair of golf carts waited beside the helipad. They were chauffeured by two Amerindian men in black shorts and shirts with small Venezuelan flags embroidered on the breasts.

"They're loyal but stupid," Rincon said to her as they approached the carts. He didn't seem to care that both men were within his hearing. He gestured towards one of the carts. "Pedro here will take you to the guest villa, and he will drive you wherever you need to go while you are here. I'll see you at the main house in thirty minutes." He climbed aboard the second golf cart, and the driver pulled away.

Beatrix watched the vehicle rattle away up the track towards the compound, then tossed her own bag into the other one and climbed in beside the driver. The cart jerked away, and Beatrix braced herself with a foot on the door frame as she studied the driver's impassive face.

"I'm Helen," she said. "Nice to meet you."

He smiled. "I am Pedro."

"You get many visitors here?"

"Yes. Señor Rincon is a very good host. We have had many very important people here."

They passed through the security gate into the compound. The guard in the sentry box looked up from his book and nodded at Pedro as they passed. Security was lax, Beatrix noted.

They glided through immaculate gardens that were filled with the smell of the delicate orchids blooming in the flowerbeds. Beatrix noticed tiny jewel-coloured humming-birds darting between the blooms and smiled.

"It's a beautiful place," she said. "How many people work here?"

"Señor Rincon has many people on his household staff, mostly women from the town, as well as his drivers and security men."

"How many security men are here at the compound?"

Pedro was thoughtful. "Fifteen," he said. "More when the minister visits or we have a special guest."

"What can you tell me about them? Are they Amerindian, like you?"

Pedro shook his head. "Not like me. They are white men mostly. They live in the barracks behind the warehouse, but they do not talk to the others. If you want to know about them, you should talk to Señor Brown—he is in charge."

She sat back in her seat. Fifteen men wasn't a lot to take care of the gold mine, she thought. And from what she had seen, they clearly weren't preoccupied with guarding the compound. They were so remote here that Rincon must have felt secure. She thought about the threat that he had described from Fuego de la Muerte and wondered whether he had overplayed it to get her to come out here.

The golf cart pulled to a stop outside the bungalow she had seen from the air. Pedro jumped out and took her bag.

"Welcome to El Corazon De Oro. Come—I will show you where you will stay."

"There's no need," she said. "I can manage."

He looked crestfallen. "Are you sure?"

"Yes. I can manage," she said again, more gently this time. "But could I call you if I need a ride into town later?"

He brightened. "Absolutely. Use the house phone and ask for me. It will be my pleasure to drive you, Miss Archer."

"Thanks, Pedro," she said, returning his smile. "I'll do that. And please—call me Helen."

His smile broadened. "Thank you, Helen. And if you please, my name is not Pedro. I am Francesco."

She raised an eyebrow. "But Señor Rincon said—"

"Señor Rincon calls all the men from the town 'Pedro.' He says it's easier than remembering our names."

Beatrix shook her head incredulously. She already thought Rincon obnoxious, but he continued to surpass himself.

"Francesco it is, then," she said taking the bag. "As soon as I get settled in, I'll give you a call. I'd love to get a closer look at Prosperidad while I'm here."

The bungalow was tastefully furnished and spacious. There were toiletries in the bathroom and groceries in the fridge. Beatrix dropped her bag in the kitchen and popped a beer while she toured the rest of the bungalow. The rear of the house opened onto a wide deck with a kidney-shaped pool and a barbecue set large enough to roast an ox. She closed the sliding doors to keep out the insects and went into the main bedroom. Laid out across the bed was a stunning red cocktail dress and a handwritten note from Rincon suggesting that she would look wonderful in it, and hoping that she would honour him by wearing it to dinner.

She stared at the note. Not only did Rincon want her to kill for him, he wanted her to look attractive at the same time. She was beginning to think that his hiring her was little more than fulfilment of some sort of fantasy. She wondered if Fuego de la Muerte was just a figment of his childish imagination, too. But she reminded herself that Rincon was important to Michael's plans and that she had to be tolerant. She would be patient, but she was damned if she was going to dress up for him like some showgirl he could show off to his friends.

She stuffed the dress out of sight at the bottom of the wardrobe. Then she opened her case and took out a pair of denim jeans and a T-shirt along with a pair of soft-soled loafers that would be quiet if she wanted to take the opportunity to look around.

Her research on Rincon had been brief, but it suggested that he was a man of few surprises. The puff-piece in *El Nacional* made it clear that he believed women should satisfy themselves with motherhood and keeping the house, and that business was the domain of men. An interview in *Notitarde* painted him as a playboy and included a photo spread of him with younger women on his arm like expensive accessories.

She finished dressing and went to the window. A limousine had pulled up at the larger house, and a distinguished-looking couple were climbing into the car as the driver loaded their bags into the boot. The car had government plates. Beatrix guessed that it belonged to a judge or a senior minister.

She was curious. What could be so attractive about Rincon's hospitality that his guests would be willing to undertake a four-hour drive all the way from Bolivar?

TWENTY MINUTES PASSED before there was a knock on the front door of the bungalow. Francesco was outside.

"Señor Rincon requests the pleasure of your company on the rear veranda. May I escort you?"

They took the golf cart to the main house. It was even more impressive up close, with five or six thousand square feet across two storeys and walnut double doors at the front. Shrubs and topiary had been expertly trimmed into abstract shapes around the perimeter, and an antique-style lantern was suspended above the porch.

A smiling maid showed Beatrix into a hallway the size of a railway ticketing hall with acres of white marble flooring and a red-carpeted staircase that swept up to the top floor. Large oil paintings were arranged up the staircase, most of which seemed to be of Rincon: sitting by a fireside, mounted on his polo pony or dressed in hunter's clothes and carrying a large shotgun. Beatrix felt certain he had never done any of these things himself.

"This way, please, Señora."

The maid led her down the hall through an open-plan living room to a large veranda at the rear of the house featuring picnic benches and coffee tables, enclosed by gossamer-fine mosquito netting.

Rincon sat alone at the largest of the round tables, nursing a bottle of aguardiente. He smiled when he saw her, but the expression quickly turned to a frown. "You have not changed."

"I'm fine like this."

"You didn't like the dress?"

"I'm here to sort out your problem, Señor Rincon, not to go dancing."

Rincon frowned again and reached for his lighter to cover his irritation. He was silent for several seconds while he coaxed his cigar back to life. She could see her rejection had annoyed him, and this pleased her.

He recovered his equilibrium quickly, though Beatrix noted a slight tetchiness in his voice as he asked her to sit.

A houseboy arrived with a silver salver.

"A drink?" said Rincon. "Gin and tonic, perhaps? We have many to choose from."

"Mineral water."

"You refuse to drink with me, too?"

"This isn't a social visit. I'm here to work."

He shrugged and helped himself to a gin and tonic, then instructed the houseboy to bring her a bottle of mineral water. "A shame. I've never had much time for denying myself life's pleasures. I've worked hard for my success, and I like others to enjoy it with me. You saw the limousine outside?"

"With government plates. You had important visitors."

"An important minister and his wife. Powerful people, and good to have as friends. Most senior members of government have visited me here at some time or another."

Beatrix was tiring of his boastfulness. "Shall we talk about work?" she asked as the houseboy returned with a bottle of water and a glass filled with ice.

"Always the professional," he said, giving her a smile that did not reach his eyes. "What would you like to know?"

"You said the mine was being attacked."

"Yes. The attacks began about eight months ago. Three local men were shot to death up in the mountains—two Indian guides and a priest named Father Jair Beltrano. The priest worked at the local medical centre in Prosperidad. We found his satchel beside the river. We think Fuego's bandits shot him and threw him over the waterfall."

"They never found his body?"

"The waterfall is over two hundred metres high. If there was anything left of Father Beltrano by the time he hit the bottom, the piranhas would have picked it clean."

Beatrix frowned. "And what makes you so certain that Fuego did it?"

Rincon made a show of spitting on the deck. "Because he and his men are godless communists. Killing a Catholic priest in a country like this is an unthinkable crime. Only someone who cared nothing for God, or the rule of law, would do such a thing."

"And the other attacks?"

Rincon looked evasive. "Sabotage at the mine. Prop shafts removed, winches and pulleys cut through."

"Is that so serious?"

"It disrupts our work, and it costs me money." Rincon looked irritated now. "And that is not all. Some of my security patrols have been attacked at night; one of my men was shot in the leg. My trucks have been vandalised so that I am unable to transport the ore. Then, last month, as I mentioned earlier, three men in masks held up the payroll office."

Beatrix took a sip of her water. Something about Rincon's story was troubling her. From the briefing Michael had given her, it had sounded like Rincon's mine was virtually under siege. But this sounded like nothing more than the sort of low-level crime and petty vandalism suffered by any large corporation.

"What makes you so sure this is all being done by the same person? Those crimes could have been carried out by any number of people."

Rincon drained his glass and signalled to the houseboy for another. "There is only one man behind these outrages —Fuego de la Muerte and his gang of cutthroats. Ask the people of Prosperidad if you doubt me. Some of them believe he is some kind of champion come to defend the rights of the common man."

"Robin Hood?"

"Who?"

"Stealing from the rich to give to the poor."

"Yes. Exactly that."

Beatrix took another sip of water. "A modern-day Robin Hood doesn't sound like something you need to hire me for. Maybe you just need a few more guys on security."

Rincon held out his glass for a refill and gave her a cynical smile. "That is because you do not understand the way that poor Venezuelans think. Most of the poor are too stupid or lazy to work their way out of poverty. Instead, they imagine someone like Fuego de la Muerte will come and liberate them. You have to understand, Helen, that what I am fighting here is not just a local bandit—I am fighting a *myth*."

"Fine," she said. "I'll start my investigations in the morning. I'd like to speak to anyone in Prosperidad who might have known the priest. Perhaps if we knew what he was doing on the mountain, we might find a clue about who would want to kill him."

"Very well. I'll arrange for you to talk to my head of security."

"Mr. Brown?"

"Yes—Garrett Brown. How do you know that?"

"Your driver told me his name."

"He can tell you about their encounters with Fuego. I'll put his team entirely at your disposal."

Beatrix could imagine the type of men who would take a security contract in a place like this, and could guess how they might feel about being placed 'at her disposal.' If her instincts were correct, her meeting with Brown might prove awkward.

"I'm also going to need some equipment. What do you have by way of weaponry?"

Rincon's expression turned to one of childish delight. "I

think we can surpass your expectations. As well as a full armoury for my security team, I have my own collection. You'll find enough guns and ammunition here to start a small war."

"Why would you need that? You said the locals liked living in Prosperidad."

He chuckled. "There is a saying here, Helen. 'Put your faith in God, but carry a big gun.'"

6

The entrance to Rincon's basement was sealed by a steel door with a digital keypad. Rincon blocked her view with his body while he punched in the code.

"You are honoured," he said as the door swung open and he reached for the light. "The only people who have ever been down here are me and my head of security."

She followed him down a narrow flight of stairs to a low-ceilinged basement of raw concrete and harsh fluorescent lighting. The room appeared to occupy the entire floor plan of the house, the space divided by concrete support pillars. To their left was a gun range with targets hanging from wire pulleys at varying distances. Every other wall in the basement was filled with racks of AR-15s, hunting rifles, sniper rifles and shotguns of every imaginable calibre. There were glass cabinets filled with nine-millimetre pistols, revolvers and even Second World War automatics.

Beatrix gave a wry curse. "You weren't kidding."

She took down one of a pair of inlaid Winchesters and

worked the breech before squinting along the iron sight, getting the feel of the gun's heft against her shoulder. It had been oiled recently; presumably Rincon employed someone to take care of the weapons. She couldn't see him doing it himself.

"Help yourself to anything," he said. "I'll see you are fully stocked with ammunition and any kit you need." He turned to another cabinet and took out something chunky on a hanger. "A Kevlar vest, perhaps? They are excellent quality, but I can't persuade my men to wear them in the heat."

"I think that might be overkill. I'll wait until I know better what I'm dealing with."

Rincon gave a shrug and returned the vest to its hanger. Beatrix concealed a smile. She was not about to turn up to her first meeting with Garrett Brown in a Kevlar vest if his men had refused to wear them. That would not do her credentials any good whatsoever.

Rincon showed her the rest of his collection, which included night-vision goggles, smoke grenades and even a collection of antique garrottes made of fine wire with teak handles. She was examining a large-calibre Glock when she caught sight of an old revolver. She stared at the weapon for several seconds before lifting it from its stand and feeling its weight.

Rincon came close and looked over her shoulder approvingly. "The Colt Python," he said. "Double action handgun chambered for the .357 Magnum cartridge. It has a blue steel, six-inch barrel with walnut grips. A masterpiece in handgun engineering. You have good taste."

Beatrix turned her full attention to the revolver. She snapped open the cylinder and inspected the chambers.

Then she checked the sights and cocked and released the trigger.

"The forcing cone is a little loose," she said. "But probably not enough to affect accuracy."

"You know your guns. But, if you'll forgive me, this weapon is a little heavy for a woman, is it not?"

Beatrix gave him a cool look and then turned the grip towards him. "Load it up. I want to see if it shoots as well as it looks."

Rincon moved to a steel cabinet and removed a box of ammunition. He beckoned her to follow him to the firing range and loaded the gun with six heavy slugs.

"There you are," he said, placing the weapon down on the counter. "Let's see what you can do."

Beatrix picked it up and hefted it, feeling its solid weight. She looked down the range. There were six lanes, each one with a standard silhouette target set at fifty feet. Each target was suspended from a cable pulley by a metal clip.

Beatrix took up a stance, feet apart with a double-handed grip. The gun weighed as much as a claw hammer. She took careful aim and heard Rincon draw in a breath. She squeezed the trigger. The Python's blast echoed around the raw concrete walls. The steel clip holding her target to the wire immediately pinged away down the range, and the paper sheet fluttered to the floor.

Rincon chuckled. "Your aim is a little high," he said. "But that is understandable. It's heavy."

Beatrix did not reply. She took aim at the target in the next lane and fired again. Once again, the clip spun away and the target fell to the ground. Four more shots exploded in quick succession. Each time, the bullet struck the target's supporting clip.

As the last paper target folded gracefully to the floor,

Rincon gave a small gasp of surprise. "The clips... You *meant* to hit them..."

"I hit what I aim at, Señor Rincon. Every time." She put the hand cannon on the counter. "Have it sent to my room with two hundred rounds and a tactical holster. Then call security and tell Garrett Brown I'd like to see him."

7

I t was less than five minutes before Brown showed up at the house. He was short but powerfully built, his sweat-stained T-shirt tight over his muscular torso. He wore a wide-brimmed cowboy hat and a Bowie knife strapped ostentatiously to his thigh.

Chewing a matchstick, he climbed the steps of the veranda with the sort of swagger Beatrix recognised from some of the soldiers she knew. He didn't sit, choosing instead to cross his arms and lean against one of the supporting posts.

He nodded to Rincon, then eyed Beatrix suspiciously. "Is this her?"

He spoke with a strong Australian accent.

"Helen, this is Garrett Brown—my head of security."

Beatrix nodded. "Mr. Brown."

Brown removed the matchstick from between his molars. "No one calls me Mr. Brown except my lawyer. I'm either Garrett or 'boss.' Take your pick."

Beatrix gave him a half smile. "I'm pleased to meet you, Garrett."

Brown moved away from the post and pulled up a chair, turning it around and straddling it so that he could lean on the back. "Rincon tells me he wants my boys to report to you."

Beatrix stiffened. Brown clearly wasn't the type to waste time getting to the point. That was good; the sooner they got this out in the open, the better.

"Is that a problem?"

Brown shrugged. "Don't worry about me. But some of the boys... they'll need some persuading to take orders from a Sheila."

"Then I'd better introduce myself."

Brown grinned. "Great. How about straight after we're done here?"

"That works for me."

"What did you want to see me about?" Brown said, turning to Rincon.

"Helen wants to know about Fuego."

"That right?" Brown turned back to Beatrix, eyebrows raised.

"It is," she said. "What can you tell me about him?"

Brown shrugged. "Not a lot to tell. Fuego and his blokes hit a couple of my patrols out in the forest. They put sugar in the diesel tanks and got away with the safe from the count-house. All small beer, but bloody annoying. I reckon he's just a peasant farmer with a few guns behind him. He's a pain in the arse, but nothing we can't handle."

Beatrix glanced at Rincon. "I understand that the locals think he's a bit more than that."

Brown snorted. "The locals. They're as thick as the shit they wade in. You can rob a bank, beat your wife and murder whoever you like, but as long as you go to church on

Sundays, the locals think the sun shines out of your arse. Trust me, Fuego's a nobody." He turned to Rincon. "Just give me a week and I'll find him and skin him alive for you."

Rincon frowned. "We have already discussed that. He's run rings around you, so I hired Helen to take care of it. I expect you and your men to show her every courtesy."

Brown narrowed his eyes but said nothing. Beatrix realised that this was a battle of wills that had been going on for some time before she arrived. She tried a different tack.

"What can you tell me about the priest?"

"Father Beltrano?"

"Why would Fuego want to kill someone like that?"

She saw a glance pass between Rincon and Brown. "Who knows? Fuego's gang probably thought the priest had something worth stealing. And the old fool had it coming. He should never have been on that part of the mountain. The old mine workings are dangerous for anyone who doesn't know them."

Beatrix sighed. She would just have to play along for now until she could turn up something more concrete on Fuego, but already this was starting to feel like a wild goose chase.

"I'd like to talk to some of the villagers in Prosperidad who've seen him."

"They won't talk to anyone they don't know."

"Maybe. Can you drive me there in the morning?"

Brown shrugged again by way of an answer.

"First thing," she said, getting to her feet. "Now, let's go meet your men."

"This way."

～

Brown got up and headed down the veranda steps. Beatrix glanced at Rincon and then followed the Australian, with Rincon close behind.

A group of men were lounging at the side of the house. They straightened as soon as they saw Brown approaching, watching Beatrix carefully. There were ten men in total, all of them from the same mould as their boss. They wore jeans and checked shirts and baseball caps or cowboy hats. They were muscular and carried themselves with the same arrogance. Most wore sidearms, and two were carrying AR-15s.

"Listen up, lads," barked Brown. "This here is Helen Archer. She's the outside help that Señor Rincon has brought in to sort our little Fuego problem. I'm told she's hot shit."

The men began to laugh.

"What's your plan, lady?" called out one of the men. He wore a thick moustache and stood about six feet five, with the build of a mountain gorilla. "A honey trap?"

They laughed. Beatrix stepped forward and eyed each man in turn. "I want to make some enquiries in the town. Someone must know who he is or where he's hiding. If we turn up any useful intel, I'll want to organise a hunting party. I'll let Señor Brown know when I need your help."

"Horseshit!"

Beatrix turned to look at the man with the moustache. He had stepped out of the group, and now he stood facing her with his with feet apart and his hands on his hips.

"You have a problem with that?" Beatrix said coolly.

"I do."

"What's your name?"

"Dingo."

"Go on, then. What is it?"

Dingo turned to Brown. "Since when do we take orders from some skinny blonde bitch who wouldn't know the jungle if it bit her on the arse? Which it will." He swung his gaze back to Beatrix. "We're professionals, sweetheart."

"So am I."

"You ever seen any action?"

Beatrix held his gaze. "Enough."

Dingo took another step forward. "Bullshit."

Beatrix glanced quickly at Brown and then at Rincon. Brown stood with folded arms and an amused expression, while Rincon clenched and unclenched his fists, and his eyes glittered with excitement. She could expect no help from either of them. They both meant for this scene to play out.

She turned her attention back to Dingo. He was at least twice her weight and heavily muscled; she knew she stood no chance in a straight contest. He stood with his arms held away from his body, his eyes wide and his weight poised over his toes.

"You like disco?"

Confusion passed across Dingo's face. "What?"

"That moustache."

"What about it?"

"It's very Village People."

The others laughed. Dingo took another step forward. His fists were clenched now, and his jaw jutted out.

"There's no shame in it," Beatrix went on conversationally.

"In *what?*"

"Things have changed. Attitudes. It's good that you don't have to hide it."

He lunged at her.

Beatrix knew he was coming and was ready. Her leg snapped out, and her instep connected hard with the big man's groin. He doubled over, and she brought her knee up into his face. She heard the crunch of bone as Dingo fell sideways onto the grass.

One of the others came at her now. She deflected the punch with her forearm and stepped to the outside, hyper-extending the man's arm and pulling it down hard over her shoulder. There was another crack as the man's elbow splintered. He screamed in shock and pain.

The remaining men took a step back. Dingo struggled to sit up. No one moved to help him. The second man was squealing, and the crotch of his trousers was wet with urine.

Brown stepped up. "Show's over, shit-heads. Someone get Alonso to the doctor and see that his arm is fixed. Take Dingo, too. The rest of you—get back to work."

The man called Alonso was helped up and led away, still sobbing at the mess that had been made of his arm. Someone else helped Dingo to his feet. He managed a last half- hearted glare at Beatrix before he limped away after Alonso.

Beatrix noticed that Brown was staring at her. His condescension was gone. Now he looked at her as though he had uncovered a viper beneath a stone.

"Bloody hell," he said. "I think you made your point."

"I'm not here to make friends," she said. "Now, if you don't mind, I'm going to turn in."

"You don't want to eat with me?" Rincon said.

"I'd rather have some food sent over to the bungalow."

"I'll send one of the lads."

She turned back to Brown. "I want to go to Prosperidad in the morning. I'd like you to drive me so we can discuss Fuego on the way. I'll see you at eight."

Brown inclined his head a fraction without taking his eyes from her. As she walked away, she could feel his eyes boring into her back.

F rancesco arrived at Beatrix's room at seven with a trolley bearing fresh fruit, boiled eggs, toast, juice and hot coffee. On the bottom of the trolley, covered by a fresh linen napkin, was the Colt Python. It had been supplied with a new tactical side holster and four boxes of .357 Magnum semi-jacketed, soft-point cartridges.

"You need me to drive you today, Helen?"

"Not today, thanks, Francesco. Señor Brown is taking me into Prosperidad."

The man's face fell. "Oh, I see. Helen, perhaps if I might..."

"What is it?"

Francesco wrung his hands anxiously. "If you go to Prosperidad with Señor Brown, then it is likely that no one will want to speak to you."

"Why not?"

Francesco's discomfort increased. "Not everyone believes those stories about Fuego having killed Father Beltrano."

"Do you know something about that?"

Francesco looked over his shoulder at the front door as though he expected Brown and his men to come bursting in at any moment. "I spoke out of turn. Forget I said anything."

The man was clearly terrified.

"Please, Francesco. Tell me what's wrong."

"It's just... If you go into Prosperidad, try to go alone. And while you are there, speak to Sister Magda at the clinic. She is a good woman. She will help."

"Do you know her?"

He beamed proudly. "She is my sister."

"Your sister?"

"Yes. And she is not afraid of Señor Rincon and his men. She will help you."

"Thank you," she said. "I'll make sure to speak to her."

She ate the eggs and toast, washed down with the hot coffee. The coffee was strong and rich, and it gave her the buzz she needed. Francesco's nervousness confirmed what she had already begun to suspect: there was more to the story of the priest and Fuego de la Muerte than Rincon had told her. She made a mental note to ditch Brown and seek out Sister Magda at the earliest opportunity.

She finished her breakfast and turned her attention to the Colt Python. She examined the weapon. It would have huge stopping power, but it was a heavy piece of ironmongery and would be slow to deploy, even with the tactical holster. It was a sacrifice she was prepared to make. She remembered her encounter with Brown's men; they wouldn't accept a woman doing the job without a lot of persuasion. Her display with Dingo and his mate would keep them off her back for a while, but she had no doubt the lesson would need to be repeated. The gun would be a visual reminder that she was not to be underestimated.

She downed the last of the coffee, loaded the gun and strapped the holster to her thigh.

Time to go to work.

9

———————

She found Brown waiting by the main gates to the compound in a battered Toyota pickup that was splattered with iron-red mud. He had the same wary, narrow-eyed look he had worn the night before. The inside of the truck was muddy and littered with cigarette butts. A rack in the rear held a twelve-gauge and a pair of multi-band radios hanging from webbing straps.

"Morning," he said.

"Morning."

"Where to?"

"Let's start with a tour of the area around the compound. Then take me to Prosperidad."

"Whatever you say," he said. "But you're wasting your time in the town. There's nothing there but peasants and dog shit."

They drove in silence for the first ten minutes, the Toyota bucking its way along the uneven dirt tracks. The forest had been cleared fifty feet back on either side, though there were signs it was creeping back. It must have been a full-time job for several people to keep it in check. Brown was working hard, she knew, to make sure there was nowhere for anyone to lie in ambush.

She pointed to a smaller track that disappeared through the trees. "What's up there?"

"Leads to the top of the mountain," said Brown, without taking his eyes off the road. "Nothing up there except for a few old mine workings from the last century. Dangerous. You fall down one of those pits, no one's ever going to find you."

She watched his expression carefully. "Is that where the priest was killed?"

"That was over on the other side of the mountain. Where we found the bodies of his guards."

Beatrix frowned. "I was told he was local."

"So?"

"If he was from Prosperidad, why would he walk all the way around the mountain to get to the top? Why wouldn't he just head up that track?"

"How the hell should I know? Maybe he just needed the exercise."

Or maybe he wanted to avoid being seen going up there, thought Beatrix. She could have pursued the point, but there was little to be gained from antagonising Brown. She decided to change the subject.

"You don't seem to like the people around here very much."

"That'd be fair enough. Don't let the happy, smiling faces fool you. They'll have the skin off your back for a shirt as soon as look at you."

"Not such happy employees, then?"

He turned to look at her for the first time. "They've got good employment, accommodation and medical care in a country where half of their relatives are starving to death. They get treated decently, but they still hate our guts."

"Is that why they make a hero out of Fuego? Because he stands up against big corporate interests?"

"Like Rincon?" He shrugged. "Maybe. But don't get taken in by any of that liberal bullshit about saving the rainforests and protecting the natives. Everybody here is on the take— the mining companies, the politicians, the cartels, *everyone*. Every once in a while, someone like Fuego comes along and says he's fighting for the people. He gets them all riled up about their heritage and spins them some bullshit tale about how the Pemon are all the same people and they need to preserve the old ways. Trust me, Fuego's no different from anyone else in this shithole—he's out for himself, just like every other Tom, Dick and Harry."

"Sounds like you hate it here."

"You wouldn't be wrong."

"So why stay?"

He took his hand from the wheel and rubbed his thumb and forefinger together. "He pays bloody well. More than makes up for the inconveniences."

They drove on.

"How are you going to do it?" Brown said at length.

"Do what?"

"Kill the bastard."

"I don't know," she said.

He looked at her again with something like admiration. "Doing your reconnaissance first? That makes you a real pro, not like the rest of us." She didn't rise to the bait. "How many have you got?"

She frowned. "You've lost me."

"How many have you killed?"

"Enough."

He sniffed. "Done my fair share, too. But every fucker I slotted was a danger to me or my men. It's different to you."

"You've lost me again."

"Rincon told me about you. You go after people when they're not expecting it. I don't know—seems pretty low to me."

Beatrix could have laughed out loud. "You've got standards, you mean?"

"At least I give the bad guys a fighting chance."

"Not the smartest tactic. You might regret that one day."

A stray dog scurried across the road. Brown stomped on the brakes, then drove around it.

"What about Fuego?" she said. "Who is he? Where did he come from?"

"Fucked if I know. Like I said, he's just a nobody with a gun. They call them *pistoleros*. The country's bloody riddled with them. Ex-forces guys, or police who decide to take to the forest and work for themselves. He'll be around for a few months before some other big shot makes a name for himself by taking him out. It happens all the time."

"So Rincon's wasting his time by hiring me?"

"The boss can spend his money however he likes. As long as he pays me, I don't give a fuck. As for you, I reckon you'll spend a few weeks looking before you give up and go home."

They passed a battered sign beside the track that told them they were one kilometre from Prosperidad. Beatrix remembered Francesco's advice about not showing up with Brown in tow.

"You can drop me here," she said.

He looked at her incredulously. "You want to walk?"

"I don't want to look too conspicuous when I arrive."

He looked her up and down. "A white woman with a hand cannon strapped to her thigh. You'll blend *right* in."

"Just pull in over there," she said, pointing to a spot beside the road. She glanced at the radios hanging in the back. "Do those have a full charge?"

"They're not much use if they don't," he said as he pulled over. "Help yourself."

She took one of the radios, tested the battery and then slung it across her shoulder. "I'm going to look around for a couple of hours. I'll give you a call when I need a ride back. Okay?"

Brown snorted. "It's not like I have anything better to do than run around after you."

She got out, slammed the truck door and watched him turn around and drive back the way they had come.

She started off in the direction of the town. The going was hard. The mud was thicker and deeper than she had expected, and in no time her boots were caked. The forest ran close to the edge of the track at this point, and thick clouds of flies swarmed around her head. She was beginning to wish she'd asked Brown to drop her nearer to the town, when she came over a rise in the ground and saw the ugly sprawl of Prosperidad laid out before her. It was surrounded by dense forest and overshadowed by the high cliffs that rose almost vertically out of the jungle. It had something of the Old West about it; the main track was a thick smear of red mud running straight through the centre of town, and rough concrete buildings lined the main street, painted in faded greens and turquoises. Each building sprouted lopsided balconies, sunshades, satellite dishes, aerials and air-conditioning units. A lattice of black power cables ran back and forth over the road, hanging slack from thick wooden poles. Makeshift bars and cafés had appeared in the spaces between the larger buildings, offering *arepas* and *tamales* along with cold beer and the ubiquitous Cola-Light.

Beatrix hiked the radio onto her shoulder and was about to set off when a movement caught her eye from the foliage to her right.

She turned to look. There was a *thwack*, and something smacked into a tree trunk at high velocity, inches from her head.

Instinct kicked in. She dropped to one knee, pulling the Colt from the holster and slowing her breathing. She scanned the foliage on the far side of the road, trying to gauge where the slug had come from.

Whatever it was had been nearly silent.

It didn't sound like a gun.

A second *thwack* cracked out of the undergrowth and split the leaves close to her head.

Beatrix stayed low and waited for whoever it was to give themselves away.

10

Beatrix flattened herself in the low brush and pressed her face against the dirt.

"Come out," yelled a voice in Spanish. "You are trespassing on land claimed by Fuego de la Muerte."

Beatrix clutched the Colt tighter and waited.

Another projectile whizzed through the air and struck a branch above her head.

Beatrix moved.

She surged up from cover and broke into a low run through the bushes.

Another slug smacked into a tree as she passed. She darted across the track and into the tree line on the other side of the road, immediately doubling back under cover of the foliage and moving soundlessly towards the sound of the voice. She circled around, behind her attacker, placing her feet carefully and bending branches as little as possible. As she drew closer, she could hear whispered voices through the trees and saw two heads pressed close together in the undergrowth.

"Where is she? Did I get her?"

"You missed, *idiota!* You couldn't hit a cow's arse from ten feet."

"You want I should put one in your face?"

Beatrix edged closer, then holstered the Colt and reached through the branches, grabbing both heads at the same time and cracking them together hard. There was a smack of bone on bone and a loud shriek as two small boys jumped up from the undergrowth. They whirled around to face her, clutching at their bruised heads.

"Hey! What did you do that for?" blurted one of the boys, his eyes already filling with tears.

Beatrix judged them both to be around eleven, with dark skin and black hair. They were both dressed in faded T-shirts, cut-off jeans and flip-flops. One of the boys carried a slingshot. Beatrix snatched it from his hand.

"Hey, that's mine. Give it back."

Ignoring him, Beatrix examined the slingshot. It was homemade, fashioned from a piece of wood and a bicycle inner tube. There was a small pile of smooth stones on the ground where the two had been lying. If the boy had been shooting at her with this, then his aim had been impressive.

"You think it's clever to fire stones at someone who's carrying a gun? You could have got your heads blown off."

"Not us," said the second boy. There was more defiance in his eyes than his companion's. "This is our forest. You wouldn't be able to find us if we didn't want you to."

"And yet here we are," said Beatrix, putting the slingshot in her pocket. "Which one of you is Fuego de la Muerte?"

"I am," said both boys simultaneously.

Beatrix couldn't help smiling. "There's two of you, then? And I suppose you're both responsible for the trouble up at the mine, stealing money and damaging trucks? Maybe I should report you to Señor Rincon?"

The two boys looked at each other and then at Beatrix. One of the boys shoved his hands in his trouser pockets and dug at the dirt with the toe of his flip-flop. "No, we didn't do those things."

"But we *will*," said his bolder companion. "When we're older, we're going to run away to the forest and join Fuego's gang. Then we're going to steal from that *bastardo* Rincon and give to the poor, just like Fuego does."

"I see," said Beatrix, raising an eyebrow. "What are your real names?"

The boys looked at each other again. "I'm Emilio," said the first boy.

"I am Juan."

"And where do you live?"

"Prosperidad. Where else would we live?"

"And what about Fuego?" she said. "Have you ever seen him around here?"

"My brother, Pablo, saw him," said Emilio. "In the forest, when he was looking for bush meat. He came across Fuego's camp. He said Fuego and his men have demons' faces, and if you try to kill them, you go straight to hell."

"Right. And did Pablo happen to say where he saw this camp?"

"We wouldn't tell you even if we knew," Emilio said, crossing his arms defiantly. "You're one of Rincon's people."

"Your manners could do with some improving," said Beatrix evenly. "Does your mother know the way you speak to strangers?"

Juan glared at her fiercely. "My mother is dead. She got the mine sickness and died two years ago. There's just me and my sisters now."

"What's mine sickness?"

"People die from it around here," said Emilio. "You drink

the shitty water and you get sick. My uncle Esteban got blood sores all over his body before he died."

Beatrix realised with a start that these boys were about the same age as Isabella, yet they already seemed to have a casual relationship with death. She looked around the clearing in the direction of Prosperidad. "One more question. Do you know Sister Magda?"

Emilio nodded. "Everybody knows her."

"Can you take me to her?"

"What's it worth? What will you give us?"

"I might agree not to tell Sister Magda about your bad manners. Something tells me she wouldn't like it very much."

"Fine," Emilio said. "But give me back my *tirachinas* first."

Beatrix shook her head. "You'll get it back when I see Sister Magda and not before. Shall we make a start?"

The two boys looked at each other, shrugged, and then set off through the forest, taking a narrow trail that led towards the back end of the town. Their earlier reticence quickly gave way to a natural curiosity that was centred mainly on the Colt Python.

"Is that your gun?" said Juan, ogling the pistol.

"That's right."

"Is it loaded?" said Emilio.

"Not much use if it's not."

"Can I shoot it?"

"No."

"Can I hold it, then?"

"No."

Juan made a disgusted noise and began kicking a stone along the path while Emilio studied her carefully.

"Do you work for Señor Rincon? Are you one of his *pistolas*? Sister Magda says we shouldn't talk to the *pistolas*."

"Does she?" Beatrix looked at the boy curiously. "Why does she say that?"

"She says they are bad men," said Emilio. "She says they do bad things. Sometimes they kill people. One of them shot Father Beltrano, but—"

"*Callate ya!*" Juan yelled at his friend with a suddenness that startled Beatrix. The other boy immediately reddened and fell to silence.

"Father Beltrano? The priest? I thought he was shot by Fuego."

"It's a lie!" Juan's face twisted into a furious knot. "Fuego never shot no priest. He's a good man, and I'm going to be just like him when I'm older. Then you and all of Rincon's *pistolas* better watch out."

Beatrix frowned thoughtfully. There was clearly more to the killing of Father Jair Beltrano than she had been led to believe. She would ask Sister Magda about it when she got to meet her.

11

The trail emerged from the forest onto a low rise overlooking the town's rubbish dump: a stinking mountain of burst sacks, damp cardboard and rotting food where packs of grey dogs fought over scraps. The boys led her through the foothills of the dump, unconcerned by the open sewer that ran through the centre of it. They ducked between two breezeblock buildings, down a tiny passage, and emerged onto the main street she had seen from the hillside. A market was set out along the street, and the air was filled with the shouts of stall holders selling live chickens and fly-covered meats. Women in sarongs and straw hats bartered over tired-looking plantains and breadfruits, while children with black hair and bowl cuts floated paper boats in the mud pools. A pot-bellied man wearing an over-large gold watch and a filthy apron beckoned Beatrix towards his makeshift café, where plastic chairs were set out under a blue tarpaulin. The air was filled with the smells of *arepas* frying on a hot griddle, underpinned by the background stench of human excrement.

The boys led her down the main street, weaving

between the parked Land Cruisers and the trail bikes that jostled for space on the narrow road. Beatrix's gun attracted the attention of the young men on the street corners, although hers was not the only one on show. Several men carried shotguns or sidearms. Those who did not have a gun favoured long-bladed hunting knives or machetes strapped ostentatiously to their bodies. Prosperidad looked like the sort of place where a minor misunderstanding had the potential to escalate with frightening speed.

"This is it," Emilio announced. "We're here."

They had arrived at what might charitably be called the town centre, a spot where the two widest and muddiest streets crossed at right angles. On one corner was a small chapel, made of white painted wooden slats; next to that was a low breezeblock building with a corrugated tin roof. There was a green cross over the door, and a sign read 'Centro Medico de Prosperidad.'

The two boys led her through the main doors and into a waiting area where two or three dozen people sat on cheap plastic chairs or on the floor. A young woman sat at a wooden school desk with her head bent low over a stack of paper on a clipboard. She glanced up and frowned as they came in, then went back to her paperwork.

A ceiling fan turned too slowly to do anything other than redistribute the hot air; the room was a flurry of movement as overheated patients fanned themselves with magazines and papers. The air smelled of pine disinfectant and vomit.

Beatrix put a hand on Emilio's shoulder. "Where is Sister Magda?"

"She works here—"

"There she is," said Juan.

A nun, dressed in a plain grey habit, had appeared from

behind a curtain separating off a small treatment area. Beatrix caught a glimpse of a young woman with a small baby before the curtain was drawn back.

"Sister Magda," called Emilio.

The nun looked up and frowned at Beatrix and the boys. Beatrix judged her to be in her fifties, with a severe face and a stone-hard expression. She was not surprised the boys were afraid of her. Sister Magda folded her hands into the sleeves of her habit and made her way across the cracked linoleum to where they stood.

"We brought someone to meet you," said Emilio.

"She's one of Señor Rincon's *pistolas*," added Juan.

"Why are you not both in school?" The nun's voice was as flinty as her expression, and both boys immediately fell silent.

Emilio bit his lip. "We... er..."

"We were on our way there now," Juan finished for him.

The nun's scowl deepened. Her hand flicked out of her sleeve and clipped Emilio and then Juan around the ear.

"That's for lying to a nun," Sister Magda snapped. "Get to school. And say your rosary before you go to bed as penance."

"Yes, Sister," they chorused.

The boys turned to leave, but Sister Magda called them back.

"It's nearly lunchtime," she said. "Go out by the kitchen and tell the cook I said you could each have an *empanada*."

The boys' faces lit up as they scuttled towards the back door of the medical centre. Sister Magda's frown did not leave her face as she watched them go. When they were out of sight, she turned her attention to Beatrix. The nun's gaze fixed first on the gun strapped to her leg and then moved up to her face.

"You don't look like one of Rincon's usual *pistolas*."

"I'm not," said Beatrix. "At least I'm not one of his security guards."

"But you carry a gun like they do."

"I've been hired to help Rincon with a problem."

"I see. Who are you?"

"Helen Archer."

"And what does that have to do with me?"

"Your brother Francesco said I should talk to you. He said you might be able to help with my enquiries."

Sister Magda snorted contemptuously. "That idiot brother of mine is too helpful for his own good. What was it he thought I could help you with?"

Beatrix noticed that several people were looking curiously in their direction. "Is there somewhere private we could talk?"

"You can say what you want out here. I have nothing to hide."

Beatrix shrugged. "Fuego de la Muerte."

The nun had one of the stoniest expressions Beatrix had ever seen, yet her eyebrows jerked up. She looked around at the waiting room and then back at Beatrix. "We can talk out the back," she said quickly. "But you need to be quick. We're short-staffed as it is."

Beatrix followed Sister Magda through a pair of doors at the back of the building and out into a small yard that was mostly dead grass with a rusted child's swing set in the middle. On the far side of the yard, steam and cooking smells poured from a small kitchen hut, and to their right stood a low corrugated iron building that Beatrix took to be an animal shed of some kind.

"Do you run this medical centre by yourself?" said Beatrix. "How do you manage?"

Sister Magda folded her arms defensively. "Some of the women in the town help me with nursing duties and cooking meals for the patients. And we have a doctor who comes from Bolivar every few weeks. It's hard work, but we manage. We have to—without this place, the people of Prosperidad would have nothing."

"Does Señor Rincon pay for it?"

The nun looked taken aback. "Did Rincon tell you that?" She laughed bitterly. "No, he pays for nothing. He takes, takes, takes from these people, but he gives nothing back."

"I thought he paid for the accommodation and care of his employees."

The nun snorted. "Rincon's idea of 'accommodation' is to give each new family a square of mud and let them build a house out of whatever they can find. He pays them in company notes that they can only spend in his own shops. As for medical care, we do what we can to patch up the broken bones and crushed limbs from the mine. The church pays for most of it, and we make up the rest with whatever small donations we can gather from the people."

Beatrix knew she shouldn't have been surprised at the extent of Rincon's shameless exploitation, let alone his boastfulness. "I didn't realise things were that bad."

"Why would you? You're white and well fed, and you're not from here. It's not your fight." She glanced back through the doors of the medical centre. "Now, if you don't mind, what is it you came to see me about?"

"I'm sorry. Rincon says he's been having problems with a local bandit."

"Fuego de la Muerte?"

"Yes. He's hired me to sort it out for him."

"I know what that means," Sister Magda said. "There are enough young men in the cemetery who were 'sorted out' by Rincon's men. But you are wasting your time if you expect to catch Fuego."

"Why?"

"Because Fuego de la Muerte does not exist. He's a story created by people who have nothing else to hope for. They imagine someone who will save them from the things they cannot control."

"And it's not true?"

She shook her head. "No more than wishful thinking."

"But what about the attacks on the mine? The sabotage, the theft from the payroll office?"

The nun shrugged. "This is Venezuela. There are banditos behind every tree. Rincon's trucks were probably vandalised by his workers, and the payroll money was most likely stolen by some criminal Rincon forgot to pay off."

"Emilio and Juan told me one of their brothers had been to Fuego's camp. They said he'd seen Fuego."

The nun gave a dry laugh. "Emilio and Juan are not the most reliable of witnesses."

Beatrix considered the nun carefully. Something about her was off; she couldn't shake the idea that she wasn't telling her everything. "If Fuego doesn't exist, then who killed Father Jair Beltrano? One of Rincon's guards told me Fuego shot the priest up on the mountain."

The nun's eyes flashed with anger. "Father Jair was my friend," she snapped. "And I don't appreciate people telling lies about him. If you really want to know who shot him, then maybe you should start by talking to Rincon. Which one of his men told you that?"

"Garret Brown."

"I thought so."

Beatrix frowned. "Brown had something to do with it?"

The nun bit her lip and turned away. "I'm not accusing

anyone. Nobody knows who killed Jair. Forget I said anything, and forget this nonsense about Fuego. The people here are poor and ignorant. They've convinced themselves there is a hero living in the forest who will protect them but, trust me, there's no one. No one except for vultures like Rincon waiting to pick their bones clean."

"Rincon seems convinced that Fuego exists."

"Rincon is a lecherous old man. Perhaps he hired you because he likes the idea of having a beautiful woman with a gun on his payroll."

"Maybe," Beatrix said. "Thank you for your help. Would you mind if I take a look around before I leave? I'd like to talk to—"

"*No.*" The nun's eyes flashed. "I've tried to be courteous, but Rincon's *pistolas* are not welcome here. I must ask you to leave now." She turned toward the gate leading out of the yard and reached for the latch.

Beatrix was about to argue, but before she could speak, she heard a high-pitched scream.

It was the sound of a child shrieking in pain.

12

The scream came from the corrugated shed.

"What was that?" Beatrix said.

Sister Magda looked agitated. She glanced nervously at the rickety building and then at Beatrix. "Nothing," she snapped. "No concern of yours. Please—it is time for you to leave."

She grasped Beatrix's arm and tried to pull her away, but Beatrix shook her off.

"It didn't sound like nothing. It sounded like a child."

The fight went out of Sister Magda, and she stepped back and lowered her eyes. Beatrix strode towards the shed, paused at the entrance, then ducked inside.

The first thing that hit her was the stench: vomit and excrement and human sweat. It was overpowering, amplified by the heat and the airlessness of the room. As her eyes adjusted to the light, she made out a line of old metal hospital beds crammed close together in the narrow space. Each bed contained a child.

One of the women Beatrix had seen in the medical centre sat beside the bed of a young girl, pressing a damp cloth to her forehead. The girl's skin was pale and clammy; her face and shoulders were covered in abscesses the size of a man's palm, each oozing blood and pus almost as quickly as the woman could sponge it away. The girl must have been about twelve or thirteen.

Just a bit older than Isabella.

"This is Ciara," said Sister Magda's voice softly as she arrived behind Beatrix. "Both of her parents were killed in a mining accident. She came to us about three months ago when the sores started."

Beatrix swallowed hard. "What's wrong with her?"

"We don't know for sure. Poisoning of some kind. Heavy metals, we think. Arsenic and possibly cyanide."

Beatrix stared at the nun. "From the mine?"

"Where else?"

Sister Magda smiled down at the child and laid a hand on her forehead, speaking to her in a low voice. The girl was desperately weak, but she managed to return the smile.

Beatrix stepped back from the bed. She was beginning to feel ill.

"Do all these children here have the same thing?"

"Not all of them. Some have cancers. We have no drugs, not that I think they would do them any good. Others suffer constant vomiting or seizures, or they simply waste away in a matter of weeks." She looked at Beatrix with sudden concern. "Are you all right?"

"I'm fine." Her skin felt clammy, and for a moment she thought she might faint.

"Come," said Sister Magda, taking her arm.

Beatrix allowed herself to be led outside and then leaned back against the wall of the building, sucking in greedy gulps of air. She closed her eyes, feeling the sunshine on her skin.

Sister Magda held her by the arm. "It can be overwhelming if you're not expecting it."

Beatrix opened her eyes and wiped her mouth with the back of her hand. "How long?"

"Before they die? Weeks. But there will be others to take their place."

"How many others?"

"Nearly a third of the children in Prosperidad have symptoms."

"And the mine is the cause of all of this?"

"What else could it be? The mine uses many toxic chemicals in the extraction process. We think the waste is polluting the water. Rincon denies it, of course. He says all of the waste is safely captured and that there's no way he is responsible."

Beatrix glanced back through the doorway. "But if you had evidence of what was happening, the authorities would shut it down. Couldn't you get samples to be tested?" She stopped as a realisation struck her. "That's what the priest was doing. He was up in the mountains taking samples."

Sister Magda watched her. "Yes. Father Jair spent several months collecting water and soil samples. He thought if he could show that the wastewater from the mining operations was the same as the water that we drink, then he could make a case against Rincon." She sighed. "Look where it got him."

"There must be someone you can go to for help? Experts you could bring in? Someone who could give you a voice?"

"Why do you care?"

"How could I not?"

"Are you a mother?"

"Yes," she said. "My daughter is the same age as that child."

"It brings it home, doesn't it?" Sister Magda paused. "You're not like the rest of Rincon's men. None of them would care."

"I was hired to do a specific job. That's it. I had no idea about any of this."

"We have tried many times to seek justice. But this is not the West. Only the voices of the rich and powerful are heard here, and Rincon and his friends are very rich and very powerful. He is friends with a man called Rodrigo Ferdinand—the Minister for Energy and Mining. He has been a guest at Rincon's house many times in the last year. Every time we make a complaint, Ferdinand's department rejects it. It is hopeless."

"But that's just one man. There must be others."

"Before he was shot, Father Jair made contact with a politician in Ciudad Guayana. He's not powerful or important like Ferdinand, but he's someone who campaigns on environmental issues. And he has a reputation for honesty."

"So go to him."

"We tried. After Father Jair was killed, two of the men from the town took the evidence we had to Guayana to see if we could get this man to help us. Everyone in the town donated money they couldn't afford to cover their travel expenses."

"And?"

"The men never arrived," she said. "Rincon heard about what was happening, and word was passed to Ferdinand. Their car was stopped at a roadblock twenty kilometres outside Guayana, and they were shot by the police. The official explanation was that they were suspected of being banditos, and that the police feared for their lives. Lies, of course. There was no investigation. They left nine children between them."

"What about the evidence?"

"Gone," said Sister Magda. "The water samples, the assay reports, the medical records. Gone. Everything Father Jair had collected was taken."

Beatrix checked her watch; it had been nearly two hours since Brown had dropped her off. She would be expected back at the compound soon.

"Can't you get more evidence? Start again?"

"We have. We have gathered fresh samples, and there is no shortage of sick people to demonstrate the effect those poisons are having. We are ready to try again." Sister Magda pursed her lips. "But none of it is any good if we can't get it to someone who'll listen. If Rincon hears about it, then the same thing will happen again. We need someone to help us. Someone strong who can stand up to Rincon's thugs." Sister Magda was staring at her.

"What? Me?"

"Why not?"

"I'm not here for that," she said.

"Ciara will die. Others will die after her. You can help stop it."

"You don't even know me."

"I can see your strength. And you are a mother. You know."

"No."

"Forget about Rincon and come and help us. It is the right thing to do."

"I can't." Beatrix raised her hands. She could only imagine what Michael would say if she told him that she had taken sides against Rincon with a group of local miners.

Sister Magda fixed Beatrix with steel-grey eyes. "You have seen what men like Rincon and Ferdinand have done here. You are perfect—they would never suspect you. I'm offering you a chance to do something positive with your life. Something meaningful."

She couldn't. If she upset Michael, then any chance of seeing Isabella again would be lost.

"I'm very sorry," she said. "I'm not who you think I am. There's nothing I can do."

"I see," Sister Magda said stiffly. "Then the mistake is mine, and I am sorry to have troubled you." She leaned forward and opened the gate for her to leave. "Good day to you."

"Perhaps I could make a donation to the clinic," she said.

"That won't be necessary. Thank you for your time. You'd best forget what we talked about."

There was nothing more to discuss. Beatrix stepped through the gate with a heavy feeling in her chest as Sister Magda closed the gate behind her. She watched the nun disappear back inside the clinic, then turned and started along the street towards the edge of town. She knew it was impossible to do what Sister Magda asked. Getting involved in a local dispute would be madness. Her priority was to finish this job and then find Isabella. Nothing else mattered.

So why did it make her feel so wretched?

And why was it that, when she tried to think of Isabella, all she could see instead was Ciara lying on her deathbed?

13

B eatrix radioed Brown to tell him that she was ready to be collected, and he arrived twenty minutes later.

"How was your sightseeing trip?" he said as she clambered into the passenger seat. "Did you get what you needed?"

"You were right," she said. "Waste of time. Whenever I tried to talk to anyone, they just clammed up."

"Told you. Those shit-waders are suspicious of their own shadows. When you've been out here as long as I have, you'll realise that you might as well talk to the fucking chickens."

Beatrix nodded. It wouldn't hurt to try to get on Brown's good side and see what information she could gather about Rincon's operation. She wanted to know if he had any knowledge of the things that Sister Magda had told her.

"How long have you been out here?" she said.

"Working for Rincon? About three years."

"Before that?"

"Mercenary. I've been all over the place. Working for

Rincon pays better, and there's a lot less to deal with, at least if you don't count Fuego."

She nodded. "That's a long time to be away from home."

"What home? I've got no family."

"No woman?"

"There's a vacancy in that department," he said. "Interested, are you?"

"Don't flatter yourself."

He laughed and, for a moment, Beatrix wondered if she was making progress with him.

"What about you?" he said. "How did you end up doing this?"

"I'm good at it," she said. "I'm not good at much else."

"You *are* good at it. You know you broke Alonso's arm? And Dingo's never going to be pretty again."

"They had it coming."

He chuckled. "They probably did." He reached into the glove box and fished out a packet of cigarettes. "So what now? You struck out in town—how are you going to find Fuego?"

"That's the funny thing," she said. "I *did* have one interesting conversation. I spoke to someone who said there's no such person. She said most of the stories are made up by poor people who want a hero to believe in." She turned to look directly at him. "What do you think? Do you think Rincon might have got this all wrong and brought me here on a wild goose chase?"

Brown's jawline hardened. "You think we just made him up? Fuck you. Who else put a bullet in Luca's back when he was on patrol six months ago? He's paralysed from the chest down. Who cut the brake lines on the ore trucks at the mine? And who was it who did *this*?"

He pulled his leg out of the footwell. He was wearing

cargo shorts now, and Beatrix saw the jagged line of angry scar tissue that ran all the way around his lower leg. The scar was thick, and his calf muscle was distorted where the line crossed.

"What happened?"

"Man trap. Seven months ago. Fuego and his animals left it on the trail where they knew we'd be. Nearly took my leg off. And that's not all—we've found grenade traps in the trees. One of the boys even found a claymore. It's a good job it didn't go off, or it would have taken out half my lads. So don't try telling me he's not real."

They rolled on through the forest in silence. Brown seemed to be just as convinced that Fuego was real as Sister Magda was that he didn't exist. Who was telling the truth?

"Why didn't you tell me any of that yesterday?" she said.

Brown didn't answer.

"Look, Garrett. I don't want to be here any more than you want me to be here. But if Fuego is real, then I need to know everything you know. That's how I get the job done and get out of your hair."

Brown took a deep breath and let it out again. "We started seeing the signs eight or nine months ago."

"What signs?"

"Carved into the trees. On all the trails around the far side of the mountain." He reached into his back pocket as he drove and pulled out his phone. The truck weaved as he flipped through his photos and then handed it to her. "Like this."

Beatrix studied the photo. It showed a symbol that had been cleanly carved into the bark of a tree. A small triangle pointed upwards and, beneath that, a circle had been filled in with deep cross-cuts.

"What does it mean?"

"They're forest signs," he said. "The Kamarakota and the Piaroa use them. The triangle is an elemental sign. It stands for fire. The circle is the sign for death. Combined, they mean Fuego de la Muerte. Fire of death."

"I need to see for myself," said Beatrix, handing him back the phone. "I'd like to organise a patrol over the far side of the mountain. I'll talk to Señor Rincon as soon as we get back."

"Not today. He's taken the helicopter to Guayana to pick up a houseguest and bring him back here. They're having a dinner party, and the likes of us are definitely not invited. Talk to him tomorrow. Stay out of the way tonight."

She settled back in her seat. "Who's the VIP?"

"Someone from the government. A minister, I think. Rodrigo Ferdinand."

14

———

By the time they arrived back at the compound, the preparations for the dinner party were in full swing. The houseboys had swapped their polo shirts for white dinner jackets. They hurried in and out of the house, bearing vases of fresh-cut flowers, crates of champagne, and trays of hors d'oeuvres on beds of crushed ice. A group of musicians were unloading guitars and amplifiers from a van that, Beatrix suspected, had driven all the way from Bolivar. Gardeners were tidying beds, mowing lawns and sweeping the paths until the compound began to resemble a five-star resort.

"Rincon's really pulling out the stops," she said as they climbed out of the truck.

Brown collected the radios and slung his rifle across his shoulder. "Ferdinand is important. The boss likes to make him feel special. I've got to put on three extra patrols tonight and, thanks to you, I'm short two men."

"Want a hand?"

She hoped that joining one of Brown's security details might give her an opportunity to do some snooping. It would be good to understand how deep Rincon's relationship with the minister really went.

Brown quickly put paid to her plan.

"You can help by going to your quarters and staying out of sight. The boss doesn't want anyone going near the minister. And forget that idea you had about sneaking out to have a look later. My lads won't stand on ceremony if they see anyone in the grounds who shouldn't be there."

"Even me?"

"Especially you. They don't like you much —remember?"

She caught sight of a Land Cruiser pulling up at the back of one of the service buildings around the perimeter of the compound. Two men got out carrying rifles. She recognised one of them as Dingo. He wore a thick strip of white plaster across his nose, and even from this distance she could see that he had two black eyes.

Dingo opened the rear door of the Cruiser and pulled out two young men. They were dressed in the thin cotton clothes and flip-flops that most men in Prosperidad wore. She could see they were young, no more than fourteen or fifteen, and both looked very frightened. Dingo and the other man began to usher them towards the house.

She jerked her head in their direction. "What's going on over there?"

Brown retrieved a duffel from the back of the Toyota and glanced towards the young men. "Party favours," he said. "Nothing that need concern you. Get to the bungalow and stay there. We can talk about Fuego in the morning. Until then, if anybody asks, you've seen nothing."

She watched him stalk away in the direction of the guardhouse, then wandered towards the bungalow, taking it slow so she could take in what was going on. She watched the two boys disappearing into the house. It didn't take a genius to work out what was going on. The closer she looked, the more Rincon's operation looked like something she really had no interest in being involved with.

She needed to speak to Michael.

15

_____

B eatrix let herself into the bungalow and conducted a routine sweep of the rooms. The small slivers of paper she had inserted in the door jambs had all been disturbed, as had the strands of hair that she had stuck across the desk drawers. The room had been searched, but not with any great expertise, probably by one of Brown's goons.

She opened the small fridge in the kitchen and took out a cold beer, at the same time retrieving her iPad from the bottom of the salad compartment where she had hidden it. She sat out on the veranda and typed out a message to Michael.

>> We need to talk.

She sipped her beer and considered what she had learned. Rincon's operation was rotten to the core: the environmental destruction, the wanton disregard for safety and the political corruption that permitted it to exist were horrific, but not unusual for this part of the world. It was clear that the people of Prosperidad needed someone who could help them deliver the justice they so desperately needed. But this was not her battle to fight, nor one that she could possibly win.

The bigger puzzle was that of Fuego de la Muerte. If Sister Magda was right and Fuego was no more than a figment of the town's collective imagination, then she would have the perfect excuse to get out of Venezuela on the next plane. But if Brown was right and there really was a bandit on the mountain, then Michael would expect her to stay and finish the job. Either way, she was going to need more information to help her make a decision, and there was only one place she could get that.

Her thoughts were disturbed by the arrival of Rincon's helicopter flying low over the compound as he returned with his guest of honour. From her window, she watched as a small fleet of golf carts streamed through the gardens in the direction of the helipad, returning shortly afterwards laden with luggage. Rincon was in one of the lead carts next to another passenger. She could not see him clearly at this distance, but she caught a glimpse of a pale linen suit and a Panama hat. It could only be the minister.

There was a knock at the door, and when she answered, she found Francesco standing outside with another trolley.

"Good afternoon, Helen," he said. "Señor Rincon was anxious that I should bring you some lunch."

She watched as Francesco removed the silver cloche to reveal a meal of fried fish, rice and fresh *arepas*, with side dishes of vegetables. There was also a bottle of chilled white wine that appeared to have been imported from France; more for the impression it gave than the taste, she thought.

"Enjoy your meal," Francesco said, setting the food out on her dining table. "My sister-in-law, Margarite, made the *arepas* fresh this morning. They are the best in Prosperidad."

Beatrix tore a piece from one of the still-warm corn

breads and dipped it in an accompanying bowl of salsa. The bread was light and slightly salty, and the spice in the salsa burned her mouth, stimulating her taste buds and reminding her just how hungry she was.

She sat down at the table and started to eat. "So," she said, through a mouthful of fried fish, "is the offer of a guided tour still open?"

Francesco paused in the task of uncorking the wine and smiled at her. "Of course. It would be my pleasure. Would you like to see the town?"

"No—I was there this morning. I was thinking I'd like to get a look at the gold mine. Would you drive me up there?"

He frowned. "Are you sure you wouldn't rather ask Señor Brown? I'm sure he or one of his men would take you. I could ask him for you if you like?"

"I'd rather that no one else knew where I was going. Can you keep a secret?"

He paused, then nodded. "I have to take the truck to fetch vegetables from the market early tomorrow morning. I could take you up to the mine on my way. Is six o'clock too early?"

"Perfect."

She guessed that there would be few people up and around in the compound to see her leaving at that time. With luck, she would be back before Rincon and Brown had even realised she'd gone.

She tasted the wine and winced.

"Is it not good?"

"It's corked," said Beatrix, pushing away the glass. "I think Señor Rincon would have been better off with a South American bottle."

"Señor Rincon insists on the most expensive wines for his guests."

She looked at him and thought again about her conversations from earlier.

"Can I ask you a question?"

"Of course."

"What do you think about these stories of Fuego de la Muerte? I spoke to Sister Magda, and she thinks he doesn't exist. Then I spoke to Señor Brown, and he says Fuego has attacked his men and left signs in the forest. Which of them is right?"

Francesco's eyes went wide. "He is definitely real. But it is best not to talk of such things."

"Why not?"

"Because... I do not believe Fuego is of this world. He is a demon in human form."

Beatrix almost laughed out loud before noticing how serious and fearful Francesco looked. "There aren't any demons, Francesco. What makes you say that?"

Francesco studied her for a moment. "I have seen him."

Beatrix sat up straight. "Where? When?"

"A few months ago," he began. "Señor Rincon sent me to Bolivar to pick up some of his favourite cigars. It was a long drive, and I was returning late when the truck broke down in the forest about fifteen miles from the compound. I had no radio to call for help, so I walked. I am not worried about being in the forest after dark. It has been my home since I was born. But after a while, I realised I was being watched."

"You saw someone?"

"I *felt* someone. Like a tingle on my skin. And I felt it that night, as if many eyes were watching me at once."

"What happened?"

Francesco swallowed and reached for a glass on the table. He poured mineral water into it from the bottle on the table and gulped it down before continuing. "They stopped me about five miles from home. I came around a bend in the track, and they appeared out of the trees—twelve of them. They wore long garments that covered their bodies and heads. The leader was Fuego. He wore a hood so I couldn't see his face, but when he spoke to me, his voice..." Francesco trailed off, and there was several seconds' silence before he continued. "It was terrible. It was the voice of evil."

"What did he say?"

"That that part of the forest belonged to him. That trespassers would be hanged from a tree. I begged him not to kill me. I got down on my knees in front of him and begged for my life. In the end he spared me, but he took all the money I had, as well as Señor Rincon's cigars. Señor Rincon was very angry about that when I returned." He paused and stared into the middle distance. "Before he left, Fuego said to tell Rincon that he was going to drive him out of the forest and send him to hell." He swallowed hard. "Then he removed his hood and stared into my eyes. I shall never forget it. It was not the face of a man at all. It was the face of a devil. That's what I believe. The devil is alive, and he has come to the forest to lay claim to Señor Rincon's soul."

16

————

Beatrix sat alone on the veranda, watching the shadows creep across the gardens. Francesco's tale had put a new spin on the Fuego story. Despite what Sister Magda had said, there was clearly someone in the forest calling himself Fuego and who was creating enough mayhem to worry Rincon and his men.

As for the story of the demon? A mask, perhaps, or possibly just Francesco's overactive imagination. Either way, she hoped that her trip to the top of the mountain might shed some light on the matter.

She checked her iPad again. Nothing from Michael. She snapped the cover shut in frustration. Michael had been known to leave a message unanswered for several days before responding. His way of letting her know who was boss.

The lights came on in the main house, spilling oblongs of yellow light across the grass. A number of limousines were arriving now, some with government plates, their muddy flanks testament to the rough journey they had made from the city. She heard a band begin playing a collection of salsa tunes, along with the rising babble of polite conversation.

The party had begun.

She sipped her beer and wondered what shady deals might be getting done over the wine and canapés. Then she thought of the two terrified boys she had seen being herded into the house: 'party favours.'

She thought of Isabella again.

SHE CHANGED into black jeans and a black shirt, slipped silently over the railing of the veranda and hurried into the deep shadow of the jacaranda trees that skirted the lawns. She paused there briefly, listening for any sign that she had been spotted. Rincon had such a large ego that it would never occur to him that she might decide to spy on him. But Brown was a suspicious type, and she wouldn't have been surprised if he had posted a man on the bungalow to watch.

Nothing stirred save for the hissing of the lawn sprinklers. When she was satisfied that she was alone, she began to move through the undergrowth, keeping out of the pools of light from the main house and taking a wide detour around the guardhouse at the front gate. She felt the comforting weight of the sheathed blade that she had tucked into her waistband. She had elected to leave the Python behind; if she was caught, she would claim to be taking a late-night stroll before bed. Carrying the hand cannon would make that a little harder to believe.

She peered at the guardhouse and made a quick dash across the gravel driveway to the cover on the other side.

She was barely halfway across when the electric gate gave a clanking jolt and began to roll open on its steel tracks. Beatrix ducked quickly into the nearest bushes and crouched low as a pair of headlamps swung into the driveway and a dark limousine crunched past her on the gravel.

She was about to move when the door to the guard-house opened, and a broad figure was silhouetted in the doorway. The man stepped outside and lit a cigarette. She had a brief glimpse of the face, illuminated by the match, and saw the white plaster stuck across the bridge of the nose.

Dingo.

He flicked away the dead match and then strode across the driveway towards her. Beatrix tensed: had he seen her? She reached behind her back and grasped the handle of the knife.

The big man paused at the edge of the bushes, barely five feet from where she was crouching. She heard the scrape of his zipper, then the sound of his urine spattering over the leaves. She held her breath until he zipped himself up again and returned to the guardhouse.

She reached the far side of the house. One entire wall was given over to sliding glass doors that led onto a raised veranda. Inside the brightly lit room she could see fifteen or twenty well-dressed men and women in evening wear. The men all had startlingly white teeth and wore linen suits with silk shirts. The women glittered with jewellery. White-coated waiters moved through the group, pouring champagne and serving canapés. She saw Francesco among them, offering a jug of fresh orange juice. Rincon was in the centre of the room, waving his hands expansively as he

regaled a group with some story or other. A young woman
whom Beatrix hadn't seen before laid a hand on Rincon's
arm and seemed to find his story hilarious. Beatrix guessed
that she was being paid for her time.

On the other side of the group stood a tall man who was
as slender as Rincon was stout. He listened to Rincon with a
smile that was more polite than amused. He had an air of
importance about him. She had Googled Ferdinand before
coming out and recognised him from the search.

The glass windows were shut to maintain the air-conditioning, and the salsa band in the corner of the room was
now in full swing. There was no prospect of hearing any of
the conversation.

But now might be a good time to investigate the rest of
the property.

She continued her circumnavigation of the house. The
next room along was dimly lit by a desk lamp on a roll-top
desk. Dark, leather-bound books lined the wall. A laptop lay
open on the desk, giving off a faint blue glow. A look
through Rincon's hard drive might prove useful. She
glanced up at the tall windows and wondered if he was in
the habit of locking them.

Taking a quick look in both directions, she vaulted
neatly over the rail onto the veranda. She tugged tentatively
on the handle of one window and was pleased when it
began to slide open noiselessly. She was about to slip inside
when the office door swung open suddenly, and the main
light snapped on. She recrossed the veranda in two strides
and leapt noiselessly back into the darkness, pressing
herself into the shadows beneath the balustrade.

"... it's a fucking *curse*, Rodrigo." Rincon's voice. "The
communista are like vermin. Did you know only last month a
delegation from the mine came to see me? They were

looking for free healthcare. Not cheap healthcare, mind —*free* healthcare. These people would steal your piss if you let them."

"Speaking of piss," said Ferdinand, "have you got a proper drink? That champagne you serve is like battery acid."

Rincon laughed. "I know—it is. A hundred and fifty dollars a bottle and it tastes like it came out of a cat. Still, the women seem to like it." There was a rustle of movement and the rattle and clink of glass. "Antioqueno? I have a supplier in Bogotá."

"Perfect."

Beatrix heard liquid being poured into a tumbler.

"So," Ferdinand said, "I'm sure you didn't bring me in here just to drink aguardiente. What's on your mind?"

Rincon chuckled. "Why don't we take our drinks outside?"

Beatrix heard the glass door slide open and two pairs of footsteps crossing the deck. They stopped directly above her hiding place. Beatrix looked up and saw the outline of the two men leaning over the rail: the squat figure of Rincon and the more elegant outline of Ferdinand.

"You didn't invite me here just for steak and bad champagne," the minister said. "Let's get to the point."

"I wanted to discuss the retainer."

"That you owe."

"I know," Rincon said. "And I'm sorry it's late. I was hoping we might be able to renegotiate."

"I don't think so," Ferdinand said.

"Half a million a month is too much."

"For the political cover you need? It's a bargain. And it's what we agreed."

"It's too much."

"Do you know how difficult it is to make sure you keep your licence? The price is the price. If you don't want to pay it, I can go elsewhere. There are others who will."

"Please, Rodrigo. I've always been grateful for your assistance. But you know times have been difficult for me lately."

"You have a gold mine. How can it be difficult?"

"We've been through this. The main seam is running out. I need time for exploration."

"That's just more of your bullshit. I don't have time for it."

"The geologists came last month. They surveyed the mountain and confirmed everything I suspected."

The tall man leaned in closer. "So, what? It's true?"

"One of the richest seams in South America is right at the top of my mountain." He laughed. "There are a few logistical issues to take care of, but nothing I can't handle. Trust me—we're going to be richer than Satan."

Ferdinand was silent. Then he began to laugh.

"Well, that *is* good news. I could use the money to buy a little more influence in the Senate. A presidential run, perhaps."

"President? Imagine what we could achieve *then*. No one would mess around with a friend of the president."

"And this is why you want to delay the payment?"

"The geologists were expensive."

"Fine. You can have a month's grace. But you pay twice as much next month."

"Thank you, Rodrigo. I'm grateful."

"You're lucky I'm in a good mood."

There was another pause, interrupted by the sound of liquid being poured into glasses again. "There was something else I wanted to discuss with you," Rincon said. "I have a few security problems."

"I heard about that. Fuego de la Muerte."

"Yes."

"Running rings around your security. Is that going to cause us a problem?"

"No," he said. "I have it under control. I've brought someone in to take care of it. A friend of Michael Yeung."

"I warned you not to deal with him. My protection won't extend that far."

"It's just a little business on the side. I provide the ships he needs to deliver his merchandise to the South American markets."

"What merchandise is this?"

"Methamphetamine," said Rincon. "Forget the coca, Rodrigo. Meth is what they want these days. There's money to be made—a lot of money."

"As a delivery boy for the triads?"

"No. I've learned from him. Now I plan to compete."

"You're going to make meth? Are you serious?"

"Why not? I've seen his operation. All you need is the right chemistry and a place to manufacture it where the authorities won't bother you. It's perfect here. We're isolated, we can use the old tunnels for production, and we have the trucks and ships for distribution. We can undercut him inside three months. After that, it's all pure profit."

"And what is it that you want from me?"

"Protection. I need to make sure we have no unexpected visits from the safety inspector, and I need the police kept away."

"How much will you give me?"

"If you can provide me with a guarantee of non-interference, I'd be prepared to cut you in for ten percent of the new business on top of our existing arrangement."

"*Please*. The monthly rate plus fifty percent."

"You're cutting off my legs. I have capital outlay and production expenses. You don't—it's just profit. Twenty."

"Forty or you can organise your own protection."

"Thirty," Rincon said after a long pause. "Thirty percent, but no more."

"We have a deal."

"But," Rincon said, "for that I need your help with something else. The bandit, Fuego—I need that *cucaracha* out of my hair before we start production."

"You said you had one of Yeung's people here for that."

"I did. But I'm beginning to think I've wasted my money. Brown tells me she's more interested in the locals. I need some real muscle to take care of this problem. Government muscle."

"A squad of Carabineros?"

"Precisely."

"I can arrange that."

"Thank you."

"Do you think it is wise to have a triad employee here while you think about undercutting the triads?" Ferdinand said.

"I've already considered that. I'll have Brown take care of her and then drop the body down a mine shaft. Yeung might ask what happened, but we don't know."

"Then it's all agreed." Beatrix heard the chink of glasses as the two men knocked back their shots. "So," said Ferdinand, smacking his lips, "what else do you have for me this evening?"

Rincon laughed. "You will not be disappointed. Two pretty young boys from the village."

The two retreated from the veranda. Beatrix waited until she heard the sound of the glass doors sliding shut before she relaxed, easing the stiffness from her muscles as she unfolded herself from the shadows.

Shit, she thought. *Now I* really *need to talk to Michael.*

17

The following morning Beatrix was up as the sun was starting to break through the forest canopy. She strapped the Python to her thigh, dropped two oranges from the fruit bowl into her backpack and stepped outside.

The floodlamps above the guard post were still lit even though it was daylight. There was no sign of activity, even from the household staff. She noticed that all of the limousines from the night before had gone, most likely departing in the early hours. Clearly only the most important VIPs like Ferdinand were granted the honour of staying at the house.

She took a shortcut through the trees towards the service area at the back of the compound where the jeeps were kept, startling brightly coloured birds into the air as she went. The jungle was a beautiful place despite the ugliness that people like Rincon brought to it.

She was frustrated that there was still no word from Michael. She needed to tell him about the conversation she had overheard last night and about Rincon's plans to undercut his business dealings. She was sure Michael would abort the mission, and she would be away from the compound in a matter of hours. Either way, she had no intention of still being there when Brown invited her to go out on patrol with his men. Rincon had made it clear last night that it would be a journey from which she would not be returning.

She was pleased to see there was no sign of Brown or any of his men in the service area. Not that he worried her— she knew she could take him on—but the need to be sociable when she knew what was planned was more than she could manage at this hour of the morning.

She found Francesco fresh-faced and smiling as he stood proudly beside an ancient pickup truck that appeared to be held together with tape and baling wire. Unlike all the other vehicles in the compound, this one was spotlessly clean and mud-free, and he was polishing it carefully with a rag. She suspected he might have got up early just to clean it for their journey.

"Good morning," he greeted her. "A beautiful day."

"It'll do," she said. She flung her backpack into the back of the truck and hauled herself inside. "Don't know why you're bothering with that," she said, indicating the rag. "The truck will be filthy again inside a hundred yards."

"We all pick up some dirt along the way," he replied cheerfully, folding the rag into a pocket. "But at least some of us start out clean."

She smiled at his good nature as he clambered into the driver's seat and started the engine. "Where would you like to go? The waterfalls are very beautiful."

"I'm not here to be a tourist. I want to get a better sense of the mountain. I still want to see the mines."

Francesco made a face. "If you say so, but there's not much to see there—just mud."

She clutched the handholds as the truck turned onto a rutted track at the back of the property, and they were immediately engulfed by the canopy. She looked back as they left the compound and was pleased to see there was still no one around. She was confident her departure had been unnoticed.

"Tell me," she said after the compound was safely out of sight, "does Señor Ferdinand visit here very often?"

Francesco shifted into a lower gear as the muddy track sloped sharply upwards. "About once a month. He and Señor Rincon are business partners. They've known each other for a long time, I think."

"What about the gold mine? Is it profitable?"

The truck fishtailed briefly in the mud, and Francesco wrestled to get it back under control. Then he shrugged. "Not profitable enough for Señor Rincon."

"What makes you say that?"

"He always gets very angry when he visits the mine. He shouts at the foremen and says they are lazy and taking his money for doing no work. Lately, his anger has become very great. My wife's brother works at the mine office. He says the mine has been losing money. Everybody in the town is afraid they will lose their jobs if the gold runs out."

Beatrix frowned. That sounded very different from the conversation she had overheard the night before. "Are you sure that's right? Has Señor Rincon not said anything about the discovery of a new gold seam? Somewhere near the top of the mountain?"

Francesco shook his head. "I don't think so. I would have heard if that were true."

Beatrix settled back in her seat. If Rincon really had

found a rich new deposit of gold, why wasn't the news all over town?

Francesco ground the gears as he attempted to coax the ancient vehicle up the muddy path. Beatrix glanced nervously down into the steep ravine that dropped away into the jungle on the passenger side. The truck nearly toppled several times as Francesco navigated the steeper sections. Beatrix realised that if they started rolling, there would be little to stop them until they reached the bottom.

Finally, the trail flattened out and emerged from the dense jungle into a clearing. The sun was now over the tops of the trees and already demonically hot. Beatrix wiped the sweat from her eyes and squinted in the harsh light. She could still see the ravine on the right-hand side of the clearing, an almost sheer drop made up of loose scree.

Francesco pulled the truck to a halt at the very edge and applied the handbrake. "It is not far from here."

They climbed down, and Beatrix put on her aviators against the harsh sunlight.

As she adjusted the glasses, Francesco suddenly threw his arm across her chest. He shoved her backwards and pointed urgently at the undergrowth where she had been about to step. A fat, diamond-patterned snake lay coiled in the leaves at her feet. It had a sharp, pointed head, and it watched her with yellow, slitted eyes. Beatrix instinctively took another step backwards.

"Venomous?"

"That is a lancehead. They are very bad. They kill many people."

She watched the snake slither away into the trees. "Thanks."

Still keeping a wary eye on the spot where the snake had been, Francesco led her across the muddy path to the edge of the ravine. At the bottom of the slope, a hundred metres below them, was a tall chain-link fence, and beyond it lay the main pit of El Corazon De Oro.

Once again, the sheer size of the mine took her breath away. She estimated it was about a kilometre long and half as wide, a steep-sided pit that had been gouged out of the earth. Huge terraces had been cut into the rockface all around the perimeter, each level narrower than the one above so that the mine resembled an inverted wedding cake. She could not see the bottom of the pit from where she stood. Everywhere she looked, she saw mud. The wide tracks and the tiered stone walls of the mine were all thick with yellow slurry. High-pressure hoses blasted the walls, releasing torrents of run-off that poured over the tiered ledges in a muddy cascade.

And then she saw the workers.

There was no way to tell them apart: men and women, young and old were all thickly coated in the yellow slime. They hacked at the walls, shovelled slurry and strained to lift great baskets of ore onto their heads. They worked ropes and hauled trucks; they lifted rocks and carried rock-laden baskets up rickety, wide-runged ladders to the surface. And then there were the guards, strutting in wide-brimmed hats and dark glasses. Each guard carried a pickaxe handle and wore a rifle slung across his back.

Beatrix saw a man slip and fall over in the ooze, his upended basket scattering ore across the path. Two guards immediately closed in and stood over him, berating him as he lay on the ground. One of the guards struck the man across the back with the pickaxe handle. When this failed to move him, both guards began to batter the man progressively harder and harder until he stopped squirming in the mud and lay still. As the guards walked away, other workers moved in and picked up the man. They half-carried and half-dragged him out of sight. Beatrix did not think he was moving.

"Have you seen enough?"

Francesco was looking at her. Her skin felt clammy, and her breath was coming in quick gasps. She realised that she had been staring.

She turned away from the pit. This was the reality of how Rincon's wealth had been made. This was the misery he inflicted on these people to pay for his big house and his fine wines.

Not your problem, she told herself. *You're leaving.*

She took a breath, then turned to Francesco. "How often does that happen?"

"How often do they beat someone like that?" Francesco shrugged. "Very often." He eyed her nervously. "What would you like to do now? Shall I take you back to the compound?"

Beatrix shook her head. "Not yet," she said. "Take me to the top of the mountain. I want to see all of it. I want to know what Rincon is hiding up there."

18

F rancesco stared at her with frightened eyes.

"I cannot take you up there. Señor Rincon has forbidden it. Besides, that part of the forest is where Fuego roams—it's where Father Beltrano was killed."

Beatrix began walking back towards the truck. "I know Rincon has forbidden it," she said over her shoulder. "That's why I want to go. Come on, Francesco. What are you afraid of?"

"Plenty," said Francesco as he hurried alongside her. "Señor Rincon. Señor Brown. Señor Ferdinand. These are dangerous men who would not be pleased if I disobeyed their orders. And I still need to get to market before the best vegetables are all sold."

Beatrix swung herself into the truck's cabin. "Don't worry. I won't tell anyone, and you'll still have plenty of time to get to market. Just drop me near the top, and I'll walk down."

"Walk down?" Francesco looked horrified as he climbed in and started the engine. "That is not a wise thing to do. Fuego is a dangerous man." He pulled away from the edge of the precipice and turned the truck towards a steep track that led up through the forest.

"I'll manage."

Francesco was silent for the rest of the journey. After about fifteen minutes, the track came to an abrupt end in a muddy turning circle fringed by forest. Francesco brought the truck to a halt and pointed to a narrow trail leading away through the trees.

"Up there," he said. "It's about ten minutes up the trail. But it is not safe. Many people have been killed, including Father Beltrano."

Beatrix checked the cylinder of the Python and then slapped it back into the holster. "Thank you."

She got out of the truck and walked away without looking back. As she entered the trees, she heard the truck pulling away down the mountain.

She was alone.

She headed along the track, skirting the deep, muddy pools and keeping a careful watch for snakes. She was surprised at how quiet the jungle was when she was on her own. Apart from the drone of insects and the occasional cry of a toucan, the humid forest air was as still and heavy as a cloak. Already the heat was like a steam bath. The damp earth exhaled a faint mist that clung to the hollows and made whorls and eddies as she passed. Her light clothing was plastered to her skin, and the sweat ran in oily rivulets; she could barely imagine what it must be like to slave continually in a gold mine in such heat.

As she neared the top of the trail, something caught her eye. Two shapes had been cleanly carved into the bark of one of the trees, a triangle pointing upwards and a circle filled in with cross-hatching. They were the same symbols Brown had shown her on his phone.

The sign for Fuego de la Muerte.

The marks still looked fresh, as though they had been cut into the wood in the last few days. It was clearly meant to be a warning. She released the restraining strap from the Colt and rested her hand on the butt as she continued.

The forest thinned out as she climbed, and the path became littered with scree and rocky debris. Tall outcrops jutted from the slopes on either side of the path, carved into abstract shapes by millennia of erosion. The mist was thicker up here, and low clouds moved silently across the landscape. It felt like an alien world, a million miles removed from the manicured gardens of the compound she had left only a couple of hours previously.

The rocky path levelled out onto a wide plain of bare rock, splashed with green and purple lichens. Spiky plants with leaves like green blades occupied sheltered niches, and shallow streams carved channels across the surface and gathered in clear pools. She peered up at the sun, which shone weakly through the mist, then struck out towards the cliffs she had seen looming above Prosperidad.

The mountain was not large by the standards of South America—barely a thousand metres tall. But it was high enough to afford an excellent view of the surrounding area, or at least it would have if the mist would clear. As she drew closer to the cliffs, the heavy boulders became less frequent and the rock became fissured and fragmented. Without warning, the ground dropped away suddenly, and she found herself standing dangerously close to the edge of a precipice as sheer as the side of any skyscraper.

The cliffs fell away like rocky battlements, dropping into a thick blanket of fog about three hundred metres below. The tallest trees poked through the top of the fog bank like green fingers. She was glad that she had decided to come up here while there was still enough daylight. Accidentally stumbling over the precipice in the dark seemed like a real possibility.

She turned away from the view and looked around. There were signs of human activity in the immediate area. A small aluminium-sided shed had been erected in the lee of a rocky outcrop, and several fifty-gallon steel drums were stacked against it. Scattered on the rough ground she saw lengths of tangled steel cable, a broken shovel and an old tyre—the sort of items that might be found in any old mine workings.

She continued along the edge of the plateau, taking care to keep well back from the edge of the cliffs. After a few minutes, she spied something that looked out of place in the barren landscape. She crouched down and moved aside some stray fronds of creeper to reveal a perfectly round and smooth-sided hole drilled down into the bare rock. When she shone her torch into it, the light was immediately swallowed by the darkness. She picked up a stone and dropped it into the hole. It clattered away down the sides, but she heard no indication that it had reached the bottom.

She frowned. Why would Rincon send people all the way to the top of the mountain just to drill holes?

Farther on, she found a second hole, also drilled into the bare rock. Scattered around the lip of it she found some tiny white pellets, round and hard like pale peppercorns. Gingerly, she gathered up a handful, jiggling them in the palm of her hand and then squeezing them gently; they were waxy and stuck together like plasticine. She sniffed them and then recoiled, her lip curling. It was a smell she knew well. She plucked several leaves from a plant and wrapped them around the pellets in her hand, then placed the little bundle in the pocket of her jeans.

She found eight more holes along the top of the cliff top, with white pellets scattered around each of them. Next to one of the holes she found a long muslin bag, with pellets clinging to the inside of it.

By the time she had finished her investigations, the sun was high in the sky, and most of the fog had burned away. She returned to the cliff and looked over the edge.

The cloud had completely burned away to reveal a sheer drop of perhaps five hundred metres down to the forest canopy. The trees continued down the steep slope for several hundred more metres until they levelled out where the forest met the sprawling mess of Prosperidad, directly beneath the spot where she was standing.

And at that moment, she knew exactly what it was that Rincon was planning.

She turned away from the cliff edge. Her heart was pounding. She thought she was hardened to the evil that men could commit in the name of greed, but this... this was something else.

As she turned to leave, the air split suddenly with a whistling noise, and something buzzed past her, barely a metre from where she stood. She dropped to her belly, seeking as much cover as she could among the low rocks. More shots came at her from a different direction now, kicking up plants and dirt a dozen paces away. One shot splintered a large rock close to her face, and she flinched as a sharp piece of stone sliced her forehead.

Rincon's men?

She glanced right and left. There must be at least two shooters. Judging from the angle of fire, they were stationed behind separate boulders about seventy metres away. They were beyond the accurate range of the Python, but that didn't mean it couldn't still be a deterrent. She pulled out the heavy pistol, raised her head cautiously above the sparse vegetation and spotted one of the shooters, his head and shoulders visible above the rock as he shouldered his rifle. Grasping the Python in both hands, she squeezed off two rounds. The second shot struck the boulder close to his face, and the man ducked quickly behind cover again.

To her left, the second shooter broke cover to get a better angle on her position. She squeezed off two more rounds in quick succession. The man let out a startled yelp and, to Beatrix's surprise, turned and ran back towards the tree line. The first shooter followed suit, breaking cover to run after his partner as they both headed for the forest.

Beatrix stood up and watched them retreat, cursing under her breath and wiping blood from her forehead. If they were Rincon's men, she had to stop them before they radioed the compound for help.

The two were nearly in the trees, too far away for the Python to be of any use. She started running, keeping the pistol at the ready. One of the men glanced over his shoulder as he entered the trees and fired his rifle wildly back at her. But it was a panicked shot, and the slug went high.

The men disappeared into the trees, and Beatrix plunged after them. The branches closed above her head, and the thick undergrowth slowed her pace immediately. She tried to force her way through the vegetation, but the going was tough, and there was no obvious trail to follow. Aside from her own rapid breathing, she could hear nothing at all. It was as if the forest had completely swallowed up the two shooters, leaving no trace that they had ever existed. She stood still, listening and looking, with the pistol at the ready.

There.

On a broad leaf an arm's length away, she spotted several drops of fresh blood. She turned her head slowly, scanning the undergrowth, her eyes narrowed. And there again—a metre or two beyond the first droplets was a smear of blood on a low-lying branch. She walked slowly on, but found no more signs that anyone had passed that way.

The dense vegetation opened suddenly into a crude clearing where the foliage had been hacked back. She stepped into the middle of the space and swept the gun in a full circle. There was no sound, no clue as to where the two men had gone. She had to face it: they had gotten away.

The movement came suddenly from her left. A hooded figure darted from behind a tree and raised something to his mouth. She dived aside as something hissed past her ear.

She fired back instinctively. The bullet went marginally high, splintering bark and making her attacker stumble backwards and drop the blowpipe he had been holding. Beatrix made maximum use of the advantage. In two strides she crossed the clearing and grasped the man by his grey robes, shoving the pistol in his face.

"Who are you?"

The man began to wail, screaming like a banshee as he cringed away from the weapon.

"Tell me who you are."

It was no good. The man's shrieking grew in volume. She was wondering whether to just let him go when she heard the unmistakable sound of an automatic rifle being cocked behind her. She whirled around and dropped her stance, bringing up the pistol in a combat grip.

Then she froze.

A dozen dark figures had emerged from the shadows. They wore the same rough grey robes as the first man, with hoods pulled up and cloth masks like balaclavas hiding their faces.

She had not heard them approach nor caught sight of them until now. It was as though they had simply materialised out of the trees. All of them were heavily armed. Most carried AK-47s that looked ancient and battered but well-kept. Several wore bandoliers across their chests and had long machetes strapped to their backs.

One of the hooded men stepped forward and jabbed his rifle at her aggressively. His meaning was clear. Moving slowly, she laid the Colt Python carefully on the ground, straightened slowly, and stepped back with her hands up.

"It's okay," she said, as softly as she could manage. "I'm not here to hurt anyone."

The man with the gun collected the Python. As he reached for the weapon, Beatrix noticed there were three fingers missing from his right hand.

He stepped back and then nodded to a figure on the far side of the circle who stood farther back in the shadows. Beatrix had not noticed him before. He was shorter than the others and carried no weapons, but he had a presence about him that set him apart.

The newcomer stepped slowly into the clearing, drawing the gaze of the others as though he were generating his own gravity. Beatrix could not see his face hidden in the folds of his hood, but she could feel him studying her. She kept her expression as neutral as possible.

He stopped within arm's reach of where she stood, and now she could see the red glow of a cigar butt smouldering within the folds of his hood. The ember reflected in his fathomless black eyes, making them glow like red coals.

"This place is *prohibido* to Rincon's people," the figure intoned. "Those who come here—they die." The voice was the dry rasp of sandpaper on brick. His lungs crackled as though he was sick.

"I'm not one of Rincon's people," said Beatrix.

The tip of the cigar glowed in the darkness of the hood. "Don't lie." He raised a hand, and immediately the others aimed their weapons at her. "You cannot deceive me. I see everything on this mountain."

"You're Fuego?" she said.

He didn't answer.

"A lot of people told me you didn't exist."

The man leaned closer and, for an instant, she caught a whiff of something rotten, as though he was decaying beneath his robes.

"Do I look real enough to you, Señora? You are Helen Archer. I know what you came here to do. You have been foolish. It will be the death of you."

19

F uego de la Muerte stared at her as if searching for signs of fear in her face.

Beatrix considered her options.

She could turn and make a run for it through the bush, hoping to lose herself in the trees before Fuego's men could open fire. It wasn't a prospect that filled her with optimism. It was unlikely she would get more than a few paces before she was cut to pieces.

She could try to talk her way out of the mess. But Fuego didn't seem interested in that.

The third option was the most desperate. She could go on the attack.

Fuego was within her reach, and she still had the stiletto tucked into her waistband. Taking him hostage might be her best chance of escape.

"Stop! You cannot kill her!"

Fuego and his men turned. A ragged figure was hurrying out of the trees. He was dressed in the same rough grey robes as the others, but without a hood. His white hair and beard were long and tangled, and he was limping heavily. "Fuego, stop—you cannot do this. She is not to be harmed."

Fuego's men stepped back and lowered their weapons. The old man ignored them as he staggered past.

Beatrix estimated him to be in his seventies. His face was heavily lined, and he held himself like a man used to carrying pain. His piercing blue eyes were clouded with anger. "You *promised* me, Fuego. You promised that if I helped, you would end the killing. Is this how you repay a promise to God?"

The other men looked down at their feet. Only Fuego met his gaze.

"She is one of Rincon's. She would kill us all."

"You don't know that. You shoot first and seek answers after."

There were several seconds of silence while the two men glared at each other. Then Fuego bowed and stepped back. "As you wish. Do with her what you will."

Fuego retreated to the far side of the clearing, and the other men gathered around him. They didn't leave, however, and Beatrix knew that she wasn't out of trouble quite yet.

The old man turned to Beatrix. "You were warned many times to stay away from here. Why do you insist on courting trouble?"

Beatrix glanced at Fuego and then turned back to the old man. "I didn't come looking for trouble," she said. "I came here looking for answers. My name is—"

"I know who you are. And I know why you are here. Do you think the arrival of a mercenary would go unnoticed in Prosperidad?"

Beatrix raised an eyebrow. "Who are you?"

The old man examined her carefully as though trying to make a decision. "My name is Father Jair Beltrano."

Beatrix blinked. "Beltrano? I thought you were dead."

"Shot—yes. But, as you can see, not dead. At least not yet."

"I don't understand."

The frown lifted from his face, and he glanced around. "I will tell you, but not here. This way."

He began to stride away through the trees. Beatrix threw another glance at Fuego and his followers and then started after the old priest. The others followed at a distance.

"I was told you and your guides were killed by Fuego," she said as she caught up with the priest. "What happened?"

"My guides were murdered in cold blood. I was shot and left for dead in the river. I'm told I went right over the waterfall, though I don't remember much about it."

"You were shot?"

"In the chest. My life was quite literally saved by the word of God."

He reached into a deep pocket of the robe to pull out a small black book, then handed it to Beatrix. It was a cheap Bible of the sort found in religious bookshops all over South America. But the pages were pulpy as though they had once been soaked, and there was a large hole in the centre of the cover. A heavy slug was still embedded deep within in the pages. She looked up in surprise at the old man.

"Your Bible stopped the bullet?"

"Mostly," he said. "It still broke three of my ribs. I also broke both my legs in the fall. I was found at the bottom of the waterfall by Fuego and his men. They carried me back to their camp and nursed me to health. It's been a long and painful recovery, but I thank the good Lord for every day of it."

Beatrix handed the Bible back to the old man. She

glanced over her shoulder at Fuego and his men. "Who shot you?"

"I think you know."

"Garrett Brown?"

"Yes, and his men. They caught me and my guides near the top of the mountain."

"You were gathering evidence for a case against the mine."

"You have been talking to Sister Magda," he said. "But, yes. Brown thought killing me would serve as a warning for anyone else who was tempted to venture up here. If it hadn't been for Fuego and his men, he would have succeeded, too."

She glanced back at the men again. "They don't look that dangerous. I mean—a poisoned dart?"

Father Beltrano held up the dart, which he had pulled from the tree bark in the clearing. It was around ten centimetres in length and made from a finely pared sliver of wood. One end was wrapped tightly with cotton, while the sharpened point was stained dark with black paste.

"Curare," he said. "Made from an old Amazonian recipe. The Indians here have used it for centuries to hunt game. A small dose like this won't kill you, but it will leave you paralysed while they decide what to do with you. Here—you can keep it as a reminder not to underestimate them." He handed it to her. "Just keep your fingers away from the sharp end."

Beatrix took the dart and inspected it briefly before slipping it into her shirt pocket, taking care to place it so that she would not stab herself by accident.

"Things can get rough up here," Father Beltrano said. "There have been several gun battles with Brown's men, but the losses have been mostly on their side. Fuego knows these forests too well to get caught out. Ah—here we are."

They had arrived at a second clearing, larger than the first. A large fire crackled in a pit in the centre of the space, and a blackened pot was suspended above the flames. More of Fuego's people sat on stones and logs around the fire, their faces and hands bandaged so that it was impossible to tell whether they were male or female. Rifles were stacked in neat pyramids around the edge of the camp, and two large field tents had been erected at one end. Some basic medical supplies were laid out on a folding table; she saw antiseptic bottles, kidney dishes and rolls of bandages.

"What is this?"

"Their home, of sorts. Fuego and his people will live here for a few months and then move on before Rincon's men catch up with them. It's a perpetual game of cat and mouse."

"And you live with them?"

Father Beltrano shrugged. "My options were limited once I recovered. I couldn't go back to Prosperidad—Brown would have killed me. I suppose I could have gone back to the city, but, in the end, I decided to stay with them and see how I could repay their kindness. I try to deliver what basic medical care I can with my meagre training." He leaned closer and examined the gash on her forehead with professional scrutiny. "That is a nasty cut. You should let me treat it with some iodine."

"There's no need."

"No, I insist. Cuts become infected quickly in the jungle. Wait here—this won't take a moment."

He hurried away and ducked into one of the field tents, leaving her alone at the edge of the camp. More of Fuego's men had arrived from the forest. They stacked their weapons before taking seats by the fire or stirring the cookpot or engaging in quiet conversation with their companions. Beatrix noticed that several were missing fingers; most had ugly lesions on patches of bare skin. One man was changing a cloth bandage from his arm, revealing angry, festering skin sores.

She became aware of someone behind her and turned to see Fuego.

"You are wondering what he is doing?" he said, pointing to the man.

"I was. What's wrong with him?"

"Nothing is wrong. It is a gift given by God." Fuego paused as a cough took hold of him, and he turned to spit something bloody into the undergrowth. Then he continued as though nothing had happened. "His gift burns our skin and purifies our souls and prepares us for an eternity in the company of His glory."

"I don't know what that means."

"We call our disease 'God's holy fire.' But you may know it by another name. The doctors call it Hansen's disease."

Beatrix's eyes widened. "You mean this is a leper colony?"

"We will not be called lepers. We are not outcasts—we are brothers. We take care of each other when no one else will."

"But why would you choose to live here? Leprosy is curable. The medicines are free."

Fuego plucked the cigar stub from his mouth. "Curable for some, maybe. But not for those of us who live on the wrong side of the law. Free medicines come with expensive questions. They are not for us."

"So, it was true what Rincon told me about the robberies and the attacks on the gold mine? That was you?"

"We steal so we can live. What we don't need, we give to those whose need is greater."

They were interrupted by the return of Father Beltrano carrying a small brown bottle of iodine and a handful of gauze. "Hold still," he instructed as he began to dab the orange liquid onto the cut on her forehead.

It stung, but she ignored the pain. Fuego drifted back to his men. There was laughter, and several of them threw dark glances in her direction as they talked.

"Who's helping you?" she said.

"Excuse me?"

"You know what I'm saying, Father. You've chosen to live with these men and to help them, but you can't be acting alone." She looked around at the tents and at the medicines laid out on the table. "How did you get the supplies? You can hardly go and shop for them yourself—you're supposed to be dead. Someone is helping you. Who?"

"Ah..." Father Beltrano straightened, and his gaze drifted towards one of the field tents. "Sister Magda," he called, "come out."

The tent flap was thrown back, and Sister Magda emerged.

"I should have guessed," Beatrix said.

"I thought you were warned to stay away," she said flatly.

"I couldn't help myself."

"You know what they say about curiosity."

"I do."

"Fuego would have filled you with bullets if I hadn't told Father Jair you were likely to come up here."

"She has a soft spot for you," Father Beltrano suggested, with a hint of a smile.

Beatrix nodded in Sister Magda's direction. "Thank you."

Sister Magda snorted, but did not reply. She busied herself by packing some of the medical equipment into a small valise. "I've left you fresh wound dressings and anti-septic cream," she said to Father Beltrano. "Store them somewhere dry this time."

Father Beltrano threw his hands up in amused surren-der. "We're in the jungle. Dry isn't always easy."

Sister Magda ignored him and snapped the bag shut. "I'll bring back some antibiotics if I can, but our stocks are running low."

"Whatever you can spare will be gratefully received." He glanced at Beatrix, then back at Sister Magda. "Perhaps if you are going back down the mountain, you could offer Helen a ride? She'll have to walk otherwise."

Sister Magda's scowl deepened. "It depends," she said. "Can you be trusted not to give us away? If you tell Rincon about this, the lives of everyone here would be in peril."

"I've already told you—Rincon isn't my employer. I don't have any loyalty to him. I won't say a word."

Sister Magda considered her for a moment, then picked up her bag. "Come on, then."

20

They left Fuego's camp with Sister Magda walking fast, in the manner of someone who doesn't want to be spoken to. Beatrix followed behind, feeling like a schoolgirl who has just been caught breaking the rules. When she looked back over her shoulder, she could see no sign of the camp. It was as though the jungle had swallowed Fuego and his men completely.

She caught up with Sister Magda near to the track that led down the mountain. An ancient Citroen 2CV was parked haphazardly in the mud, and Sister Magda was fumbling with the keys.

"Thanks," said Beatrix as they both climbed into the car.

Sister Magda turned to face her. "How *stupid* are you?"

Beatrix blinked in surprise. "I'm sorry. I didn't realise that—"

"You outsiders are all the same. You think you can pry into everything and make it your business. I tried to tell you there was no such person as Fuego, but you had to go digging around. Francesco warned you away from here, but still you had to come. Those men live every day with the fear of death. Do you think you help them by coming here and putting them at risk of being discovered?"

"I said I'm sorry. I didn't go looking for Fuego—his people started shooting at me."

There was silence while Sister Magda manoeuvred the little car around in the turning circle and started back down the track. It felt like one of the shock absorbers had gone, and Sister Magda seemed to have a knack for hitting every pothole in the road. For several minutes Beatrix had to focus on clutching her seat to avoid being slammed against the dashboard.

Finally, the road smoothed a little, and she was able to relax. The worst of Sister Magda's ire seemed to have passed, and she was now glowering out of the windscreen as she hunched over the wheel.

"How long have you been going up there?" said Beatrix.

"I started when I learned that they had rescued Father Jair. I do what I can for them by bringing food and whatever medical supplies we can spare. It's not enough, but it keeps them alive, and it soothes the worst of their symptoms."

"How did they end up there? A leper colony? In this day and age?"

Sister Magda gave Beatrix a pitying glance. "Spoken like a rich white girl. Leprosy is more common that you think. The poor suffer most."

"Why don't they seek treatment? It's curable."

Sister Magda gunned the little car around a sharp bend in the track, and the Citroen fishtailed in the mud, taking them perilously close to the edge of the drop. Beatrix instinctively clutched her seat, although Sister Magda seemed unperturbed.

"They don't seek treatment because it comes with too many questions. When I first met Fuego, I was just a novice nun, recently arrived in Prosperidad. He was one of many orphans in the town who had learned to live on their wits. He and his friends started with petty theft and then held up trucks on the highway. By the time the first lesions appeared on his skin, he was wanted by the police in four different states. He was too afraid of being arrested to seek help. When the marks of the disease became more obvious, the locals drove him out of town. He's lived up here ever since."

Sister Magda turned the little car off the mountain track and onto the wide road that led from Prosperidad.

"It's a big step from there to having a militia."

Sister Magda shrugged. "Not so big. Over time, others with the same disease came to join him. They found comfort from being together in their suffering."

"And strength in numbers when it came to taking what they wanted."

The nun's eyes flashed. "Don't be so quick to judge a man when you don't walk in his shoes. What would you have done? They had no other way to feed themselves. Under Fuego's leadership, they stole only from the mine, not from the people of Prosperidad. Anything they had left over, they gave to me or Father Jair to distribute as we saw fit."

"Robbing from the rich to give to the poor," said Beatrix.

Sister Magda snorted. "I know this looks strange to you, Señora, but you are judging from a place of privilege. Fuego has made the most of what life has dealt him. He and his men take communion from Father Jair every Sunday, and they care for each other. They are good people." She fixed Beatrix with a gaze that seemed to penetrate into her very soul. "I know what you came here to do. And I am telling you it is wrong."

Beatrix ran a hand through her hair. If Rincon discovered that she'd found Fuego, he would expect her to complete the contract at once. But whichever way she looked at it, Fuego did not look like he was the one who deserved her attention. She leaned back in her seat and sighed; it would have been so much easier to work without the stipulations of a conscience.

"What's the matter?" Sister Magda said. "Things not quite as black and white as you thought they were?"

"No," she said. "You're right. I was sent to take care of Fuego. But I know more now than I did."

"And he's not quite the monster that Rincon made him out to be."

She nodded. "I think the best thing I can do now is to leave."

Sister Magda looked at her and gave a dry laugh. "Is that it?"

"What else can I do?"

The nun turned onto the main road leading towards the compound. "What I asked of you before—deliver Father Jair's evidence to his contact in Guayana. If you help these people get justice, then maybe Fuego's people won't have to live the way they do."

"We went through this before. I can't help them."

Sister Magda abruptly pulled onto the side of the road a few hundred metres from the main gates of the compound and yanked on the handbrake. "Can't or won't?"

Beatrix reached for the door. "Thank you."

She clambered out of the car, shut the door and watched as the nun drove away, narrowly avoiding a mule cart coming the other way. Then she turned and trudged up the hill towards the compound. She knew that she couldn't kill Fuego. And common sense told her it would be madness to take sides with the people of Prosperidad against Rincon. She had been right before: her best plan was to talk to Michael and persuade him to let her leave as soon as possible.

21

S he checked her messages when she got back to the bungalow. There was one from Michael.

>> Call me.

It was accompanied by a number. She opened the hardened VOIP application on her iPad and dialled the number. Michael answered on the third ring.

"Beatrix, you've been very quiet."

It was a rebuke. He was annoyed that she hadn't reported in as soon as she'd arrived. He sounded calm enough, but it was impossible to tell what sort of mood was under that smooth voice. She had seen others misjudge that. It was not for nothing that they called him Dragon Head.

"It was difficult to talk before. Rincon is paranoid, and this compound is not exactly private."

"Have you completed the contract?"

"No," she said. "It took me a while to trace the target."

"But you *have* found him?"

"Yes. But he's not what he seems. He's..." She paused, reluctant to be completely open about Fuego and his disease. Michael wouldn't care and would probably consider it a sign of weakness if she mentioned it. "He's just a small-time bandit. He lives in the forest at the top of the mountain. He's no threat to anyone."

"Rincon would disagree. Deal with him. It's what you've been asked to do."

"No, Michael."

"What?"

"Rincon isn't being honest with you."

"What does that mean?"

"I overheard him having a conversation with one of his guests last night—a government minister."

"Rodrigo Ferdinand. I know they are close."

"Rincon said that his mine is starting to lose money. He's been looking for a new source of gold, and he thinks he's found it—a fresh seam at the top of the mountain."

"I don't see what this has to do with—"

"I went up there today, Michael. There are boreholes all the way along the cliff top overlooking Prosperidad. I found traces of ANFO scattered all around them."

"And what is that?"

"Ammonium nitrate and fuel oil. It's an industrial explosive used in mining. Rincon's got that whole mountaintop rigged with it. He's going to blast the top off the mountain to get to the new seam. He wants Fuego out of the way in case he tries to make trouble."

"I don't care, Beatrix. Rincon owns the mountain. He can blow up as much of it as he wants."

"No, he can't. The cliffs overlook Prosperidad. If he sets off that explosive, it'll bring a landslide down on half the town. He and Ferdinand are going to make it look like an accident. It all fits. They're going to get away with murder."

"*Enough.* Aurelio Rincon is an important business associate, and he has asked me to carry out a simple contract. It is important to my honour that the work be done well, so I sent you. But now you come to me with some bleeding-heart story? What do I care? It has nothing to do with me. I sent you to do a job, Beatrix, and I expect it to be done."

"There is something else. Rincon told the minister that he was going to start manufacturing methamphetamine."

Michael paused. "Really?"

"He said that working with you has shown him how much money there was to be made. He's planning to set up manufacturing in one of the abandoned mines and then use his own network to distribute it. Ferdinand will provide political cover, and they'll split the profits. He's planning to undercut you."

Beatrix waited.

"You are certain of this?"

"I am."

Another pause.

"Thank you."

"What do you want me to do?"

"The contract with Rincon is cancelled."

"So I can leave?"

"Not yet. There is something you need to do. Rincon has betrayed my trust. You know what that means. See that it is done before you leave Venezuela."

"That's not going to be easy. He's very well guarded."

"I don't want to hear that. Let me know when it is done, and we will see about New Zealand."

"Fine."

"And find out more about Ferdinand."

"I will."

The line went dead.

She closed the iPad cover with a snap and got up off the bed.

She needed to start thinking about leaving.

She went to the bathroom and washed her face and hands and changed her shirt. As she balled up the dirty clothing, she felt the oblong shape of the curare dart in the top pocket. She pulled it out carefully and was about to toss it into the trash, but then hesitated. She rummaged in the waste basket and retrieved the cork from the previous night's wine. She pushed the end of the dart into the cork and dropped it into a pocket of her backpack. Next, she strapped on the Python and found a lightweight cotton jacket. She tore open the lining of her suitcase and took out the false passport and the platinum credit card hidden inside. She sealed the documents in a Ziploc bag and dropped them into the backpack along with the spare ammunition and her knife.

She prised open the back of her iPad and pulled out the SIM card, crushing it under the heel of her boot before flushing the pieces.

She was ready.

Her plan was loose. She would find a vehicle in the compound and take the keys. Then she would go to the house and find Rincon. Taking care of him quietly would be best; she would use the knife if possible. She would hide the body so that it wouldn't be found for a few hours, long enough for her to get a good head start on the road to Bolivar.

It was a hasty plan, not the way she usually operated, but she didn't want to wait a moment longer than necessary. She took a last look around the room to see if anything of importance had been left behind, and, satisfied, she opened the door.

She paused. The grounds were unusually busy. Two of the compound trucks raced from the service area and out through the main gates, both of them full of Rincon's guards. House servants and gardeners were gathered in anxious groups, talking in low voices, and the main gatehouse was empty and unattended.

She spied Francesco hurrying across the lawn towards the house and hailed him.

He hurried over. "There has been an incident. In the forest, just outside Prosperidad. One of Señor Rincon's patrols was attacked. They returned fire and captured two banditos. They say that one of them is Fuego de la Muerte."

"Are they sure it's him?"

"Señor Brown seems to think so. He's gone up there with the rest of his men. They took a rope with them. I think they are intending to hang him."

Beatrix glanced at the house and wondered if Rincon was alone inside. Probably. This would be the ideal opportunity to kill him and escape while Brown and his men were otherwise engaged.

"Señor Brown and his men have been drinking," Francesco said. "They are very angry about what Fuego has done. It might not matter who they have caught. They will kill them anyway."

Beatrix made a decision.

"Do you know where they've gone?"

"*Si*, Señora."

"Good. Get a truck and meet me at the front gate in two minutes. I'm going to go after them."

22

F rancesco slid to a halt beside the gatehouse at the wheel of an open jeep. Beatrix vaulted into the vehicle, and the back wheels sprayed gravel over the lawn as the jeep pulled out, fishtailing out of the driveway and down the muddy road towards Prosperidad. About a kilometre outside the town, they reached a passing place where several trucks that Beatrix recognised from the compound had been parked.

"Pull over here," she instructed Francesco. He pulled up behind the last truck in the queue, and Beatrix jumped out.

"What do you want me to do?" he said.

"Take the truck back to the compound," she told him. "You don't want them to find you here."

She unfastened the retaining strap on her holster and then turned and ran into the trees without looking back. The forest closed about her like a cloak, blocking out the sunlight and immersing her in a world of deep green twilight. She could hear the whoops and hollers of Brown's men through the trees up ahead. It sounded like they had not needed to venture far into the forest before they'd found their quarry. And Francesco had been right; they definitely sounded drunk.

She paused in a small clearing, anxious not to give herself away too soon. She heard their voices.

"Tie 'im down!"

"This is what we do to murdering fucks like you..."

"Get the rope..."

As she crept closer, the shouting suddenly redoubled.

"For fuck's sake... He's running. Stop him!"

She ducked behind a tree as the sounds of crashing and breaking branches came towards her. She was barely out of sight when the bushes on the other side of the clearing burst apart, and a small boy dashed out. His eyes were wide with terror, his clothes torn, and there was blood smeared across his face.

Beatrix recognised Juan, the young boy she had met before.

There was more crashing from the bushes, and two men erupted into the open, chasing after him. Beatrix recognised them both from the compound: one was short and fat and the other lanky. They looked sweaty and angry, and they swayed unsteadily as they moved. The boy froze in place, petrified with fear, and the fat man grabbed him by the collar.

"Please," Juan cried. "I didn't mean nothing. Please don't hurt me."

"Hurt you?" growled the man. "I'll show you what I do to Fuego's people. I'll skin you alive."

He reached behind his back and pulled out a knife with a curved blade that gleamed like a claw.

"I'm n-not Fuego. I live in Prosperidad. Please let me go. *Please*." Juan was crying now.

The fat man smiled, pushed his oily hair out of his eyes and drew back the knife.

"Enough!"

Beatrix stepped from behind the tree.

The fat man scowled, confused, and then recognition dawned on his face. "Look what we've got here." He let go of the boy's arm and turned to her, leering.

"That's *enough*," she said again. "Put the knife away."

"And why should I do that?"

"Don't make me lose my temper."

The man stared at her and then burst out laughing. "You hear that, Benedicto? She thinks she can take me."

He lunged towards her, but he was slow from the drink and wouldn't have been a match for her if he was sober. Beatrix stepped forward and to the side so that the blade slid harmlessly past her body. She caught his wrist with one hand and brought the other down into the crook of his elbow to bend his arm. She maintained an even pressure on the wrist and guided the knife straight into his throat.

The fat man gave a gasp of surprise as the blade slid into his windpipe.

Beatrix turned to his companion. "Your turn."

Benedicto stared at her with wide eyes. He looked at his companion bleeding out on the forest floor, then back at Beatrix, and then bolted across the clearing and disappeared into the trees. When she was satisfied he had gone, she turned to Juan and placed an arm around his shoulders. He was trembling, his face slick with tears and mucus.

"Juan, remember me? We met yesterday."

He nodded and wiped his arm across his face.

"Tell me what happened?"

He blinked and licked his lips. "They came," he stammered. "The men from the compound. They caught me and

Emilio, and they said we'd been shooting at them. But we hadn't."

Beatrix squeezed his shoulders gently. "I believe you. Where's Emilio?"

Tears rolled down his face again. "They caught him. They said they were going to teach him a lesson the whole town would remember." His face crumpled. "I think they're going to kill him."

"Tell me where they took him."

Juan pointed through the trees. "Through there. About two hundred metres. There's a clearing where Juan and I make camp. They took him there."

Beatrix bent over slightly so that she could look the boy in the eyes. "Get back to town and find Sister Magda," she told him, forcing him to meet her gaze. "Tell her what's happened, and tell her I might need a place to stay tonight. Okay?" The boy nodded, gulping. "All right. Go!"

Juan fled through the forest.

Beatrix began to pick her way silently through the trees in the direction Juan had indicated. She could hear men's voices now, hooting and whooping, along with the sound of a small boy crying.

"Please... You're hurting me. I haven't done anything."

The boy's pleadings were met with laughter, and then she heard Brown's voice with its unmistakeable Australian accent.

"You were shooting at us. You're with Fuego, aren't you?"

"Get a rope," said another voice, laughing. "Let's string him up."

"Fuck the rope," said another. "Fetch the gas can."

She peered through the branches at the edge of the clearing. There were the remains of a campfire and several large stones around the perimeter for sitting on, not unlike

Fuego's camp at the top of the mountain. Next to the fire was a child's tent, which had been trampled into the mud.

Emilio had been stripped to his underwear and tied to a tree at the edge of the clearing. His skin was covered in large red welts. Brown and his men were gathered around him. The Australian was holding a freshly cut sapling in one hand and a bottle of whisky in the other.

"Tell us where your mates are," he said, cracking the sapling across the boy's bare legs.

The others fell about, helpless with drunken laughter.

One of them staggered to his feet, picked up a jerry can and began to slosh gasoline over the boy.

Beatrix pulled the Colt from its holster, noting the positions of the four men and the weapons they were carrying. She braced herself, intending to come out firing, when the slightest of movements in the tree branches to her right caught her eye. Silently, she turned to look—and found two black, glittering eyes staring back at her. A snake with a body as thick as her wrist began to uncoil itself from the upper branches, its tongue tasting her scent on the air. The reptile's skin was banded with a grey diamond pattern, and its head tapered to a sharp nose.

It was a lancehead, the same as the snake she had seen with Francesco on their trip to the mine.

23

Smiling, Beatrix zipped up the rucksack and turned her attention back to the clearing. The boy was sobbing and spluttering as the gasoline was poured onto him.

"What's it to be?" Brown sneered. "Are you going to tell us where to find your friend Fuego?"

He raised his hand so that Emilio could see the disposable lighter. He struck a flame and held it up.

The men fell about laughing again.

"Burn the little bugger!" one of them hollered, and the rest of them took up the refrain.

Suddenly one of them turned in Beatrix's direction. "Hey," he said sharply, holding up a hand for silence. "There's someone over there in the bushes. I heard them thrashing about."

All heads turned, and Beatrix could see Brown lower his hand. The flame on the lighter was extinguished, and he squinted into the bushes in her direction. "You in there," he barked. "Come out with your hands on your head. You've got three seconds before we start shooting."

Beatrix stepped out. "It's me," she said.

Brown gaped at her. "What the bloody blazes are you doing here?"

"I saw you boys race up the mountain and thought I'd see what was going on," she said conversationally. "They said you'd found Fuego." She looked over at the boy. "That's not him, though, is it? He's just a kid."

"I can't believe this," Brown said, shaking his head in astonishment. "She's made our job easier."

"How's that?" Beatrix asked him.

Brown began to laugh.

"Rincon doesn't like you much. He told me to take you out in the forest and put one in the back of your skull. You should've found Fuego and then fucked off."

Too late, Beatrix caught the movement from her left, but was unable to dodge the butt of the rifle that was slammed into the side of her head. She dropped to her knees on the ground, stars bursting behind her eyes, and then rolled to one side.

Dingo loomed above her. "Let me do it."

"Back off. We'll do her when I say so, and we'll do it properly. Grab her gun before she does any damage with it."

Beatrix fought to clear her head as Dingo bent down to retrieve the gun from her holster. Then he straightened. "She hasn't got it," he said.

"She'll have it somewhere. She hasn't taken it off the whole time she's been here."

"Where is it?" Dingo said, jabbing her with the barrel of his rifle.

Beatrix worked her jaw and tasted blood. Her head was beginning to clear. "Backpack," she muttered.

Dingo bent down, grabbed the backpack and yanked it from her shoulders. He began to fumble with the zips, then reached into the bag and fumbled inside. A look of surprise crossed his face before his features twisted into a rictus of shock and agony. He screamed, yanked his hand out of the bag and then shook it violently. The snake was coiled around his wrist like a cuff, its fangs sunk deep into the fleshy part of his hand.

Dingo fell to the ground. "Get it off me!"

"It's a fucking lancehead!" another man yelled out.

Beatrix lunged for the bag, pulled out the pistol and came up firing. She delivered the first shot to the underside of Dingo's jaw. She fired again, hitting the man next to Brown. She swung the pistol around to take aim again, but Brown wasn't there. She swivelled, searching for him, but then pain tore through her shoulder. She dropped the Colt and looked down to see the handle of Brown's hunting knife protruding from her flesh, buried to the hilt.

She grabbed the handle and tore it out. The pain redoubled, and her vision swam; for a moment she thought she might black out.

Brown was there, and she swung the blade at him, its tip passing him harmlessly as he ducked out of range.

"Shoot her!"

The last man raised his rifle and took aim.

The forest rang with gunfire.

The guard was hit more than once.

Brown flung himself to the ground.

The guard toppled over.

The barrage stopped.

Beatrix stayed where she was, trying to catch her breath as she looked for who had fired the shots.

Brown reached over to one of his fallen men and grabbed his discarded rifle.

Beatrix was starting to feel dizzy from the loss of blood.

Brown scrambled to his feet, turned and ran in the opposite direction from where the shots had come.

She watched him go and tried to get to her feet but immediately fell back, her legs weak. She looked down at her shoulder; there was a lot of blood.

Something moved at the side of the clearing. A grey shape emerged at the edge of the trees, dressed from head to foot in a grey robe and carrying an automatic rifle. More shapes appeared now, stepping silently out of the undergrowth.

Fuego de la Muerte moved to the unconscious boy and crouched beside him. He removed a knife from the folds of his robes and cut the thin leather strips that had been used to bind him to the tree.

He beckoned to another of the gunmen, who picked the boy up and held him in his arms. Then he walked to where Beatrix lay and knelt beside her, placing his gun on the ground.

"Twice in one day," he said.

24

"Sit down, Garrett. You make me nervous."

Aurelio Rincon had his feet up on the handrail of the veranda as he swirled a glass of dark, sugary rum and considered the fine Cuban cigar in his other hand. Cigars were a ritual with Rincon. Something to be savoured and enjoyed, preferably in silence.

Brown was spoiling this one.

"Four of my men. She went through them like they weren't there."

"They can be replaced. I've just spoken to Rodrigo to explain our little problem, and he's sending extra security. Trained men."

"My men were trained!" Brown exclaimed. "And it's your fault. *You* were the one who insisted on hiring an outsider to take out Fuego instead of letting me do it. And look what's happened."

Rincon stubbed out the cigar. "I have it under control. I've sent for someone else to lend a hand. He'll be waiting when she returns to the compound."

Brown looked at Rincon as though he had started speaking in another language. "She's not coming back."

"She's going to come back—she'll come after us both. Can't you tell? I've seen her type before. And it's *painfully* obvious that she's fallen for whatever line she was spun when she went up to Prosperidad. We can use that against her."

"How?"

"Find someone she's close to and use them as leverage."

"Did you have anyone in mind?"

"I've asked them to come and see me. You can take care of it for me. Make up for the mistakes you've made."

"Where are you going to be?"

"I'm going away for a few days. Business in Guayana City with Señor Ferdinand. Lure her back here and find out what she knows. She was snooping around the night we had the party—I had the cameras checked, and there she was, poking around where she wasn't wanted. The man who's coming will be able to loosen her tongue."

"The Colombian?"

"Arriving within the hour. Make sure he gets what he needs." Rincon heard a tap on the screen door. "Good. I suspect this is the reason Archer will be coming back. Come in."

Francesco stepped onto the veranda. "You asked to see me?"

Rincon had had to ask for the name of the man who had been helping Archer. "I did. No need to look so worried. Señor Brown is just going to ask you a few questions about what you've been doing with Miss Archer."

25

Beatrix surfaced slowly from dreams of a forest filled with blood and demons and snakes from which there was no escape. Trying to wake was like trying to swim to the surface of a lake of black treacle. She finally managed to force her eyelids to open and was greeted by stabbing needles of white light. She screwed up her eyes as a band of pain tightened around her skull.

She tried to take stock. She was lying down, in a bed. There was a dull ache in her shoulder, and her head was pounding.

But she was alive.

She opened her eyes again. A thick shaft of sunlight fell across the bed. It came from a square window with an insect screen but no glass. The sounds of children playing filtered in from outside. Sister Magda was sitting on a hard kitchen chair beside the bed, holding a damp cloth and watching her with a severe expression.

"Alive, then," she said. "Lucky. I thought you'd lost too much blood."

Beatrix tried to sit up but immediately fell back to the

pillows. She was in a small room with a hard earth floor and rough plaster walls. The only furniture apart from the bed was the chair Sister Magda was sitting on, a small chest of drawers and a table. A plastic bead curtain separated a tiny alcove containing a bottle of gas and a single ring. A plain crucifix hung on the wall above the bed, but there were no other adornments. The room was as humble as they came.

"Where am I?"

"Prosperidad. This is my room. After what happened in the forest, it was too dangerous to take you to the medical centre, so Fuego brought you here."

"Fuego's people brought me here?"

"They were grateful that you tried to save the boy. They saw what you did. They would have killed you if they thought you were involved."

Beatrix licked her cracked lips. Her mouth tasted like a small animal had been sleeping in it. "How long have I been here?"

"Three days. At first, we were sure you would die. We have very little at the medical centre to treat this sort of injury: no drugs or drips or antibiotics."

Beatrix carefully lifted up one edge of the dressing on her shoulder. The wound was long and deep, but it appeared to have been well cared for. It had been sewn up neatly with fishing line, and the area had been kept clean.

"Who fixed me up?"

Sister Magda pursed her lips tightly. "When Fuego's men told Father Jair what had happened, he insisted on coming here to treat you himself."

Beatrix sat up. "Father Beltrano came here? But that's—"

"Dangerous? Yes—very. He took a great risk. But he said it was a sacred duty. He seems convinced that you are God's messenger and that we must take care of you. He's coming back later to check how you are doing."

Beatrix gave the nun a puzzled look. "God's messenger?"

Sister Magda shrugged. "He gets some strange ideas. It's best not to argue." She got to her feet. "Do you want some water?"

Beatrix nodded. Sister Magda poured a glass of water from a jug on the table in the corner and helped her to sit up so she could drink. The water was warm and stale, but it tasted like nectar to her and soothed her dry throat. She took the glass from Sister Magda and drained it.

"Do you think you could eat?"

"I think so."

Sister Magda stepped into the alcove and spooned something from a pan into a plastic bowl.

Beatrix thought about what Sister Magda had told her. *Three days.* Michael would have expected her to have taken care of Rincon by now, and he would be agitated, to say the least, that he hadn't heard anything. What was worse, Brown's men would be looking for her now; it would make it doubly difficult for her to make a move on Rincon. She had to talk to Michael again.

Sister Magda returned with a bowl of stew, containing some vegetables and stringy meat. She handed Beatrix a spoon, and Beatrix began to eat. It was hot and fatty, and it tasted delicious. She wolfed it down, tipping back her head to drain the last liquid from the bowl.

"How are Emilio and Juan?" she asked, wiping her lips on the back of her hand.

"Scared. But they'll be all right."

She handed the bowl and spoon back to Sister Magda. "Is there a phone I could use here?"

The nun gave a dry laugh. "Do you see a phone in here?

We had a phone at the medical centre until about a year ago, when Rincon cut the lines. He didn't want us talking to anyone about conditions at the mine. Now the only phones are at his compound."

Beatrix frowned. She had not fully appreciated how completely Rincon controlled access into and out of his mine. She no longer had her iPad, either, so there was no way of getting a message to Michael. She pulled back the bedclothes.

Sister Magda stared at her. "Where do you think you're going?"

"I killed three of Garrett Brown's men, and Fuego killed another. Brown will be looking for me. I'm putting you and everyone else in Prosperidad in danger."

Beatrix stood, and her head immediately swam. She held on to the bed until the feeling passed and then straightened up. Her clothes had been washed and were folded in a neat pile at the end of the bed. She pulled on her jeans and her boots, moving carefully so as not to tear her sutures. Her T-shirt and jacket were clean, but still bore the faint brown stains from her blood. She gingerly pulled them on.

"Do you have my gun?"

Sister Magda raised an eyebrow. "Fuego and his men must have taken it when they brought you here. It will be valuable to them. You could consider it payment for saving your life." The nun watched in silence while Beatrix laced her boots. "Where do you plan to go next?"

"Not sure," grunted Beatrix, pulling the laces tight. "I just need to get away from here before Brown finds me."

"It's over a hundred miles to Guayana, and it's jungle nearly all the way. You have no vehicle."

"I'll play it by ear. I need to leave. I'm just making things worse."

A flash of anger crossed the nun's face. "It's too late for that. You think Rincon doesn't know you're here? Brown was up here yesterday. He beat three men, trying to get them to tell him where you were hiding. One of them has a broken leg."

Beatrix sat back down again. "Shit."

"You can help," Sister Magda said. "I told you before. You can make a difference."

"How?"

The nun went to the chest of drawers and lifted out a thick file folder. It was old and battered, bristling with slips of yellow paper to bookmark specific pages. She sat down on the chair and opened the file on her knee. Beatrix could see it was filled with notes, handwritten in a spidery scrawl, photographs and computer printouts on cheap tractor paper.

"This is the evidence I spoke to you about. Some was taken from Father Jair's notes. Other pieces have been collected from the people of the town. There are photographs of the conditions in the mine that were taken at great personal risk. We also have an analysis of the poisons in Prosperidad's drinking water that was paid for by the families. It is damning. If we can put this into the right hands, then we can prove to the world what Rincon has been doing."

Beatrix looked at the file. "You have someone in Guayana you can take this to?"

"There is a politician—an honest one. Father Jair says he is a trustworthy man who has helped other communities in our situation. His name is Julian Gomez."

Beatrix raised an eyebrow. "An honest politician?"

They were interrupted by a rap on the door, and both women turned to it.

"Is there another way out of here?" Beatrix whispered.

Sister Magda shook her head.

Moving silently, Beatrix took up a station behind the door while Sister Magda went to answer it. "Who is it?"

"It's me, Sister Magda. Emilio. *Please*—you have to come quickly."

Sister Magda pulled open the door. Emilio and Juan were outside.

"What is it?"

"It's Francesco," blurted Emilio. "You have to come."

Sister Magda paled, and her hand flew to her heart. "My brother? What's wrong? Where is he?"

"Señor Brown has him in the big house. He thinks Francesco knows where Señora Archer is hiding. Please come quickly. I think it is very bad for him."

26

Sister Magda rushed from the tiny house and was in the street by the time Beatrix caught up with her.

"Stop! You can't go there."

Sister Magda fought to pull herself away. "Francesco needs me. I have to go to him."

Beatrix grabbed Sister Magda by both shoulders. "It won't do any good. Brown isn't going to let you see your brother. It's me he wants. He knows I'm friends with him. He's holding him to flush me out."

Sister Magda fell to her knees and began to sob. Beatrix helped her back into the house with the aid of Juan and Emilio. They sat her down on the bed, and Beatrix poured her some water. "Sister Magda," she said calmly, "I need you to stay here."

"I can't—"

Beatrix silenced her with a raised finger. "You can't get Francesco out, but I can. I will."

"How?"

"You don't need to worry about that. But I *do* need you to be ready."

"How? What do I need to do?"

"Be ready to leave as soon as I get back. Get the car and stock it with fresh water and food. You'll need to leave and head for the city—Bolivar, maybe even Caracas. It's the only way to keep your brother safe."

Sister Magda nodded.

Beatrix turned to the two boys. "I need to get into the compound without being seen. Do you know how I could do that?"

"There's a door..." Emilio began.

"Into the warehouse," Juan said. "It's where they keep the supplies."

"Have you been inside?"

He nodded. "We've stolen food."

"The door's never locked," said Emilio. "And the guard is often asleep."

"Thank you," Beatrix said. "Now, I need you all to stay here until I get back. Are we clear?"

All three nodded meekly.

She turned to leave.

"Wait." Sister Magda rose from the bed, reached into a small cupboard at the foot of it and took out Beatrix's backpack. "Fuego's men didn't take this."

Beatrix took the bag and inspected the contents. The money was gone, but she was pleasantly surprised to discover it still contained her false documents and the knife.

27

It took Beatrix nearly an hour to reach the compound from Sister Magda's house. She stayed off the road to avoid any chance encounters with Brown's men and made her way through the thick undergrowth, climbing the steep slope that led to the fence. The going was tough, made more difficult by the fact that the wound in her shoulder was still sore. She hoped Emilio and Juan were right about the warehouse door. She was hoping that she might be able to get in and out without being seen at all.

Beatrix emerged from the trees. The fence was about twelve feet high, made of narrow steel mesh with razor wire along the top. Beatrix dismissed any thoughts she had of trying to scale it. She circled the property until she reached the rear of the compound, which nestled against the side of the mountain. She could see the garages where the trucks were usually kept; it looked like most of them were elsewhere.

She continued until she came to the place described by Emilio and Juan. The building was a single-storey corrugated steel warehouse with no windows; it straddled the fence to allow goods to be delivered directly into the rear. There was a steel rolling shutter, large enough to admit a truck, that could be lowered and locked. Next to that was the door the boys had described to her.

Beatrix pulled out the stiletto. She checked for any signs of CCTV, but there was nothing obvious. She was about to leave the cover of the trees when she was startled by a noise from down the hillside: the whine of a helicopter winding up to full throttle. She ducked back under cover as the noise rose to full pitch, and the dark shape of the JetRanger rose slowly into view. It cleared the treetops, dipped its nose and slid away across the canopy.

Beatrix had not been able to see who was inside, but knew that the most likely candidate was Rincon. That was unfortunate. She had been hoping that her work here might also have given her the opportunity to fulfil the terms of her amended contract with Michael.

That would have to wait.

She crossed to the rear of the warehouse, pressed an ear to the plain metal door, then tried the handle. It was unlocked. She slipped inside and stood still for a moment, allowing her eyes to adjust to the dimness. The warehouse was a typical prefabricated storage building. Aisles of aluminium shelving stretched away, each stacked with pallets of dry goods, tinned fruit and vegetables, tuna fish, barrels of cooking oil, bottled water and toilet paper and all the things a large house might need. The stocks were plentiful and stood in contrast to the scarcity that Beatrix had seen in Prosperidad.

She heard tinny music from a radio at the other end of the space. She held the stiletto ready and crept softly along the nearest aisle towards the sound. At the end of the row was a wider storage area filled with a rich man's toys: a quad bike, tennis rackets and a set of golf clubs. Near to that was a small glass-panelled office. The radio on the desk blared something by Gloria Estefan while a guard in jeans and a T-shirt snored loudly in a wooden chair. His head was back, and his mouth was wide open. A rifle leaned against the desk next to him.

Beatrix padded into the office. A quiet search of the file drawers uncovered a Serbian-made M88A handgun. She pocketed it and left the office as quietly as she had entered.

She searched for an exit that would let her into the compound and found a door that led to a brightly lit corridor with doors on either side. She advanced down the passageway, pistol at the ready, trying each of the doors in turn. The first two doors were locked, but the third opened into a small conference room. The room was in semi-darkness and was furnished with a boardroom table and chairs. Beatrix guessed that this part of the warehouse served as some sort of business centre for Rincon.

She stepped inside and, too late, sensed movement behind the door. Something cracked down hard across her wrist, knocking the pistol from her hand. She flung out her left arm, grabbing her attacker and pulling him forward as she smashed her right elbow against his chin. The man staggered back against the wall, and the tyre iron in his hand clattered to the floor. A second figure lunged from the shadows. The butt of a rifle struck her across the cheek and sent her sprawling to the floor, nearly blinded by the sudden pain.

The lights came on. She saw that there were four men in the room, including the two by the door. Garrett Brown stood at the far end, grinning at Beatrix as she lay on the floor. The fourth man was Francesco. He was tied to an office chair, he was wearing only his boxer shorts, and his skin was streaked with red welts. His head was bent forward, and a thick streak of blood from his broken nose had congealed in the hair of his chest.

28

The ice-cold water dragged Beatrix out of the darkness as surely as an electric shock. She came awake gasping and choking and discovered that her hands and feet had been tightly secured. She regained her breath, opened her eyes and blinked them clear of water. Garrett Brown stood over her, holding an empty bucket and wearing a smug grin.

"Hello again."

Beatrix took in her surroundings. She was in a different room, smaller, but with the same basic decor: a boardroom table and a handful of chairs. The only other person in the room was a guard standing by the door. The chair she was tied to was the same as the ones in the meeting room. She guessed that it was another room in the same facility. Her feet were tied together, and her hands were behind her, secured to the back of the chair. The rope binding her wrists was thin and cut into her flesh. She moved her wrists cautiously back and forth, testing. It was made of nylon; she thought that there might be a possibility of slipping the knots.

"Wake up," Brown said, slapping her.

"I'm awake."

"I can't believe you were stupid enough to come back."

"And I can't believe you were stupid enough to still be here."

He snorted. "Keep talking."

"You'd be wise to let me go," she said.

"The only place you're going after this is the furnace room. You've got four of my men to answer for."

Brown picked up her backpack from where someone had set it on the table and began rummaging through it. He took out the false papers, squinted at the photograph in the passport and then at her. He put it back in the pack. "You went sniffing around the medical centre, didn't you? And then one of my guys saw you heading up the mountain. Who were you talking to up there?"

"Piss off."

"Tell me and I'll make sure it's quick."

Beatrix flexed her wrists again to test the knots. There was a tiny bit of give in the rope, not much but perhaps enough for her to do something with. Without moving her shoulders, she started to covertly flex and relax, working the slack while keeping the effort from showing in her face.

"Rincon doesn't want to get his hands dirty with all this?"

"He's gone to Guayana on business. He left you to me."

"And you're as out of your depth with this as you have been with everything else since I've been here."

Brown gave her another slap, this one hard enough to make her ears ring. She smiled through the pain. *Good.* Anger would distract him.

She continued working the knots. The rope was chafing

her skin, but there was definitely more slack than there had been.

Brown raised a large hunting knife and held the edge to her neck. "If it was down to me, I'd open your throat right now."

"Go on, then."

"Later," he said. "You're going to tell us what you know first."

"It takes skill to get someone to talk when they don't want to. You wouldn't know where to start."

"I'd have a bloody good go," he said, "but Rincon knows someone who does it for a living."

He signalled to the guard, who turned and went outside. The door opened again a moment later. The man who entered was Hispanic, dressed in a well-pressed black suit, a crisp white shirt and polished black shoes. He was short and neat, with the sort of cadaverous, pockmarked look that Beatrix recognised from long-term opiate users.

"This is Señor Vincente Bello from Bogotá."

"That will be all, Señor Brown." Bello's voice was quiet and almost gentle. "Leave us now, please."

Brown looked oddly deflated. He looked at the Colombian, then at Beatrix, and then back to the man. "I've got instructions from the boss. I have to make sure this is done properly."

Bello did not appear to be listening. He placed a small attaché case on the table and opened it. "I don't allow observers."

Brown looked angry at his dismissal, but she could see that he was too uncertain of his ground to argue. "Call me if she causes any trouble," he said. He signalled to the guard to follow him and left the room, shutting the door behind them.

Bello reached into the attaché case, took out a clean piece of lint and laid it on the table. Then he took out several items and laid them carefully on the clean cloth as though he were preparing for surgery. Beatrix saw a pair of thin-nosed pliers, a dental pick, a scalpel, a packet of needles, a hypodermic syringe and a vial of clear liquid. Beatrix renewed her efforts on the bindings securing her wrists. She had created enough slack to work a fingernail into the knot. She began teasing it free. It was coming, but it was slow work.

She watched Bello as he filled the hypodermic and squirted out a small amount of liquid to clear the barrel of air bubbles. Then he leaned in close. She flinched at the sting of the needle in her neck and then felt the cold rush of fluid into the vein. Bello turned back to his work and left her alone while the drug took effect. He disinfected his instruments with a small spray of isopropyl alcohol. Beatrix tried to focus on loosening the knot, but it was becoming harder. The drug was starting to make her dizzy.

She guessed it was sodium pentothal. She had been dosed with it before at the MI6 training base in Fort Monkton. She tried to concentrate on the knot. It was stuck. She bent back a nail trying to move it, but it was no use. If she couldn't free her hands, then she would have no way of stopping what was about to happen.

She massaged one hand with the other, working the soft tendons and ligaments between the bones and relaxing her muscles in the hope that she might slip her hand through the loop. She managed to insert two fingers under the loop around the other wrist and pulled. The rope slipped an inch over the wide part of her hand but then stopped, wedged tight. Her hand was too big to fit.

Bello leaned in towards her with a penlight. He shone it

in each eye, checking her pupils. "Good," he said. "We can start. I'm going to ask you some questions." He picked up the dental pick from the lint cloth. "Each time you give me an answer I don't like, I shall insert this under one of your fingernails. If that fails to loosen your tongue, then we shall move on to something more unpleasant. Do you understand?"

She grabbed the wrist binding again and yanked hard. It moved farther this time, scraping raw flesh from the back of her hand, but still not far enough. She pulled again, straining as hard as she could within the tight confines of the chair.

She felt one of her fingers break.

She pulled again. The pain was excruciating, but she knew she couldn't stop. She couldn't hide it now, either.

Bello's expression darkened as he realised what she was doing.

Beatrix's hands came free, one after the other. She lunged out of the chair, her feet still bound together, as Bello pulled a scalpel from his case and whirled back towards her. Beatrix collided hard with him, driving the top of her head into his face and forcing him backwards onto the table. The scalpel fell away to the floor as they wrestled. She made a grab for it, but missed. Bello squirmed like a wild animal under her, and she fought to keep her balance and hold him still. She flung out her uninjured hand—and her fingers closed around the syringe. Clutching it in her fist, she drew her arm back and jammed it into his eye. Bello gave a high-pitched scream and tried to claw at his face. Beatrix pivoted on her bound feet, slipped behind the Colombian and clamped his neck in the crook of her elbow. She pulled, adding torque with her free arm, and choked him out.

When he was still, she let his lifeless body slump to the floor. The drug was starting to make her feel drunk. She knew that she would have to counteract it quickly or else she would be rendered helpless. She turned to his case and dumped everything out onto the table, rifling through his tools until she found another small clear bottle. The label read Bemegride, the trade name for methylethylglutarimide, a powerful central nervous stimulant. She found a fresh syringe, filled the barrel and jabbed herself in the arm. The liquid would work against the sodium pentothal in her system, reversing the neurological depression that it was causing.

The effect was not instantaneous, but she knew that the drug—and the pain from her broken finger—ought to be enough to keep her steady. She retrieved Bello's scalpel and sliced through the rope binding her feet. She found a larger knife in a zippered pocket inside his case and slipped it into her belt. She examined her damaged hand. A large piece of skin had been scraped away, and her little finger was twisted back at a sickening angle.

She rummaged through the debris on the table once again and found a roll of surgical tape along with a couple of pencils. She snapped the pencils to the correct length and then, gritting her teeth, popped her twisted finger back into alignment. Breathing heavily, she wound the tape several times around the finger and the one next to it, splinting it as tightly as she could bear. She examined her handiwork. It was untidy, and it still hurt, but it would have to do.

She picked up her backpack and carefully opened the door. She was in the same corridor she had seen earlier. She looked up and down, listening carefully. Nothing. Holding the knife in her good hand, she walked back to the first conference room and pressed her ear to the wooden door.

There was no sound from inside. She turned the handle slowly, holding the knife at the ready, then opened the door a few inches so she could peer inside. Francesco was still strapped to the same chair, his head slumped forward, unconscious. His eyes were swollen shut. His injuries seemed superficial, designed to cause pain more than any lasting damage.

She stepped quickly into the room, then turned quickly, knife at the ready. There was no one behind the door. She walked quietly over to Francesco and shook him gently. "Francesco," she said softly, "it's Helen. Wake up."

Francesco grunted and stirred but did not wake. She looked around and wondered how long it would be before Brown came back to check on Bello's progress. Not long enough.

She took a pinch of Francesco's skin and twisted it. The reaction was immediate. His swollen eyes opened slightly. She placed a finger against his lips.

"Shh, Francesco. It's me, Helen."

"Señora Archer?" His voice was pitifully weak. His swollen eyes opened enough to squint at her. "How?"

"Don't talk," she said. "Just listen. We have to get you out of here. Sister Magda's waiting to take you to Guayana. Can you walk?"

"I don't know." He coughed. "Please... some water?"

She found bottles of mineral water in one of the cupboards at the side of the room and poured him a glass. She knelt down and cut off the duct tape binding his hands and feet, then handed him the water. He drank greedily.

"Not too fast," she said. She gathered Francesco's clothes and handed them to him. "Here. Get into these and let's get moving."

"They asked me nothing," he said as Beatrix helped him dress. "They just took turns to beat me."

"Brown will pay for it—but we need to get a move on. I don't want you to be here when he comes back."

"He's not here."

"What do you mean?"

"One of his men came to find him. He said it was urgent. I couldn't hear any more than that, but they went outside, and I think I heard the cars starting."

Beatrix frowned. That was odd. She had been left with the very clear impression that Brown was invested in enjoying her punishment. If something had drawn him away from that, it must've been important.

"Come on," she said. "Put your arm around me."

Francesco did as he was told, draping his arm over her shoulder as she lifted him out of the chair. Then, still supporting his weight, she led him out of the door and down the corridor. They came to an external door. Beatrix kicked it open, and they stepped out into brilliant sunshine. She scanned the utility area behind the warehouse where the vehicles were usually kept; it was now completely empty.

"Looks like you were right. They've gone. Any ideas where we can find another vehicle?"

"My truck. It's at the back of the garage. The keys are under the visor."

They crossed the utility area to a garage with a vehicle lift and an inspection pit. They found Francesco's truck, and Beatrix helped him into the passenger seat before grabbing the keys.

"Let's go find Sister Magda."

29

G arrett Brown stood on the roof of the Land
Cruiser, looking down as his men herded people
out of the medical centre. Gathered in the street
before him was a scared and confused group of the sick and
injured. Several of them had to be held up by friends, while
others cradled bandaged limbs or simply sank down into
the mud, too weak to stand. One man carried a small child
in his arms. Brown wrinkled his nose. The poor of Prosperidad always revolted him. He turned away and called out
to one of the men herding the last of the sick into the street.

"Julio," he shouted, "is that all of them?"

Julio looked up and nodded. "Think so. The place is
pretty much empty now. What do you want us to do with
them?"

"I want them to hear what I've got to say."

Julio had told him that two of their men had seen one of
the banditos entering the town from the forest an hour
earlier. They were almost sure that it had been one of
Fuego's men; it might even have been Fuego himself. They

had sealed off the road, and Brown was confident that the man was still here.

"Translate into Spanish for me," he said to Julio. "I want them to understand every word of what I'm about to say."

Brown looked down his nose at the pitiful group.

"Listen up," he began. "You all know me. You know my reputation. You know I'm not the sort of bloke you want to upset."

He waited while Julio translated, and watched the group exchange nervous glances.

"Two of my men saw one of Fuego's bandits. It was about an hour ago, and that man came into town. It may have been Fuego himself. Fuego de la Muerte is your *enemy*. He damages the interests of Señor Rincon, and he threatens the mine. Anyone caught helping him will be shot as a collaborator and their property burned."

One of the men in the crowd stepped forward and shouted something up at him. Two guards clubbed the man to the ground, then kicked him while he lay there. No one was foolish enough to intervene.

When the man lay still, the guards stopped, leaving him groaning quietly in the dirt. No one came to help him up.

"Señor Rincon is your friend," Brown went on. "Your jobs depend on him. Everything you have, you owe to him. In return, he expects your loyalty. I want the bandito who was seen entering the town. Someone is hiding him. If you give him up, we'll leave you in peace. If not..."

He shrugged, then bent down and picked up the bottle that he had prepared. A rag was stuffed into the neck, and the smell of petrol stung his nostrils. Brown held up the bottle in one hand and his lighter in the other. He jerked his head towards the medical centre.

"Let this be a lesson as to how quickly things can be taken away."

He flicked the lighter. A woman screamed angrily, and two of the younger men surged forward, despite the earlier demonstration of what happened to dissenters. Brown's men shoved them back.

"Wait!" cried a voice from the back of the crowd.

Brown paused.

"You have to stop."

Brown peered in the direction of the shout. The crowd parted, and he saw the old nun who worked at the medical centre struggling with one of his guards. Brown knew the locals respected her.

"Let her through."

The nun shook away the arm of the guard and marched to the front of the group until she was looking directly up at him.

"You know about Fuego's man?" he asked her.

"Nothing!" she said.

"Where is he?"

"I have no idea. These people aren't hiding anything. They're just trying to survive as best they can. And they need that medical centre. Why don't you leave them in peace and take your war somewhere else?"

"Bullshit," he spat. "They know where he is, and they've decided not to help. They need to know that there are consequences for that."

Turning away from her, he flicked the lighter again, touched the flame to the rag and tossed the bottle onto the roof of the building. There was a tinkle of breaking glass, and the petrol ignited with a wash of heat that swept over the crowd. The flames tore into the dry leaves laid across the roof, spreading quickly to the old timbers and then the lath and plaster walls.

To Brown's astonishment, the nun swung a punch that connected with the nose of the guard and then rushed towards the fire. "Come on!" she cried to the crowd. "We have to save it. Help me put the fire out."

The crowd surged after her. Brown felt his control of the situation slipping away. He didn't have enough men if the crowd decided to turn against them. He had to end it now. He jumped down from the roof and strode towards the nun. She turned to face him just as he delivered a backhanded swipe that sent her sprawling into the dirt.

There was a roar of outrage from the crowd. Their shouting grew louder, and as one, they began to shove forward so that it was all Brown's men could do to hold them back. A rock sailed overhead and clattered against the vehicle.

Brown pulled out his sidearm, raised it in the air and fired once.

The crowd froze.

He levelled the pistol at the nun's head. "All of you—fuck off back to your houses and stay there."

No one moved.

"One!"

They stayed where they stood. Brown feared that he had crossed a line but knew that he couldn't stop now without losing face. He just couldn't.

He cocked the pistol.

"Two!"

His finger tensed on the trigger.

A flicker of fear crossed the nun's face, but she held his gaze.

"Wait! Please—for the love of God—please *stop!*"

Everyone turned to see a figure hurrying up the road towards them. He was dressed in a long grey robe with a hood that flapped behind him. His grey hair was wild, and his beard was ragged. He looked like a hermit, yet Brown thought he recognised him.

He pushed his way through the crowd and faced Brown. "Please stop," he gasped. "It was me you saw. I came to check on a patient. Please let Sister Magda go—I'm the one you want."

The nun spun around. "No, Father—please stay back."

"Father?" Brown looked at the old man, and realisation hit him like a physical blow. "You're the priest."

"I am Father Jair Beltrano. I've been living in the forest with Fuego. I've been helping them. But Sister Magda knows nothing. Please—let her go. You can do what you want with me. I don't care."

Brown knew that nothing had changed. He still had to make an example.

He took aim at the old priest.

And fired.

30

B eatrix gunned Francesco's truck towards the town, the wheels sliding in the mud. She prayed that she didn't spin them off the road into one of the deep gullies on either side. Driving was difficult, her broken finger sent bolts of pain up her arm every time she turned the wheel, and her left eye was still partially closed from the blow she had received earlier. The truck itself felt like it was on its last legs, it rattled and creaked, and the gears ground every time she changed up or down.

They rounded a bend, and she immediately slammed on the brakes. Two trucks were parked across the road in a crude roadblock a couple of hundred metres ahead. Two of Brown's men were leaning against the side of one of the trucks. As soon as they saw the truck, they tossed their cigarettes and unslung their rifles.

Beatrix ground the gears and reversed back up the road at speed, negotiating the bend until they were out of sight. She left the truck idling and jumped out, signalling to Francesco to do the same.

They stood by the side of the road, listening.

"I don't think they've come after us," said Beatrix after a while. "They're probably just there to stop anyone being too inquisitive about what's going on in town." She spoke with a confidence she did not feel.

"What do we do?"

"We'll have to dump the truck."

She wondered if there was another way into the town. As far as she knew, there was only one road in and out. She looked at the forest on either side of the track; it appeared dense in every direction.

"Can we get down the hill without using the road?"

Francesco was pale, and his breath came in short gasps. He leaned heavily on the truck for support. "Some of the old hunting paths run near here. The men use them when they hunt for bush meat."

Beatrix looked at him. "Are you sure you're okay to walk?"

He nodded and tried to stand straighter. "Yes. I have to be. My sister is there. My friends. I am afraid for what Señor Brown is doing."

Beckoning for her to follow, Francesco led her a little way down the track until he found a gap in the trees. He pushed his way through the branches, and Beatrix stepped in after him. Almost immediately it grew darker as the vegetation closed out the sky. They made their way slowly through the dense undergrowth, branches slapping them mercilessly across the arms and face, until at last, the path opened out into a discernible track trodden through the undergrowth. They walked single file, their footsteps the only sound as they headed downhill towards the town at the foot of the mountain. The path ran along the course of a stream now, and they had to negotiate slippery boulders.

"Where will this bring us?"

"The northern edge of town, behind the shanties. We can get through the back lanes to the main street and the medical centre. I need to know that Magda is okay."

The forest stopped abruptly at the edge of town. They passed a pit filled with rotting rubbish and an open sewer running behind a line of one-room shanties made of corrugated tin and plastic sheeting. A few skinny goats meandered between the houses, and bedraggled chickens pecked at the mud. There was no sign of anyone.

"Is it usually this deserted?"

"Usually these lanes are crowded," said Francesco uneasily.

Beatrix pointed across the shanty rooftops to a thick column of black smoke rising above the town.

Francesco's eyes widened. "That's the medical centre."

"Can we get closer without being seen?" Beatrix asked, keeping her voice low. "I need to know what I'm dealing with."

Francesco nodded. "I think so. This way."

They continued through a warren of twisted cut-throughs and rat runs until they came to a narrow lane that intersected the main street. The lane emerged from between a grocery store and the forecourt of a greasy workshop stacked with oil drums and the rusted shell of an old Cadillac. The oil drums provided cover from where they could observe what was left of the medical centre a hundred metres away. The crowd in front of the building had swelled to over two hundred people, and they were all staring in silent horror at the billowing tongues of flame that roared from the windows and doorway. The roof had already collapsed, and it was clear that the rest of the building was about to follow suit.

"Magda!" Francesco cried. "I have to go to her."

Beatrix held him back, shushing him urgently. "Stay down, or you'll get us both killed."

Two Land Cruisers separated the crowd from the burning building. Garrett Brown was standing on top of one, berating the onlookers, while his men held them at bay with their rifles. Brown jumped down from the vehicle and strode towards someone who was lying on the ground.

Beatrix recognised Sister Magda.

Brown pulled out his sidearm and fired once into the air. The sound of the gunshot sent a visible ripple through the crowd. Most of them began to move back; a few ran for the cover of the nearest alleyways.

Then Brown levelled the pistol directly at the nun.

Beatrix heard a cry from their left. A wild-haired old man in a grey robe was running along the street toward Brown and the nun. He ran past the end of the alleyway where Beatrix and Francesco were concealed, heading towards the medical centre as fast as his legs could take him.

"It's Father Beltrano," said Francesco.

Beatrix nodded. She could see perfectly well what was about to happen. "Stay here."

She knew she couldn't stand by and watch, but she was still without a gun. She pulled out the knife, but paused. Trying to tackle Brown and his men with that on its own was suicidal. She would be better off keeping it out of sight until she needed it.

"You two!" shouted a voice from behind them. "What are you doing down there?"

Beatrix whirled around to see a guard approaching along the alleyway behind them, an AK-47 at the ready. The sounds from the street had masked his approach, and now he was nearly on top of them.

Swift as a cat, Beatrix crossed the gap between them and

dropped to one knee, slicing the stiletto across the man's stomach. As he bent, clutching his belly, she pivoted behind him and whipped the blade across the tendons at the back of his knee. She rose from her crouch and jammed the tip of the blade through the side of his neck, piercing his throat in a short, over-arm strike. The guard gurgled and clutched at his throat as he crumpled to the ground.

She slid the blade back into her waistband, then picked up his AK-47 and checked the magazine. She yanked a spare from the man's belt and tucked it into her back pocket.

"Helen!" Francesco croaked. He was staring, wild-eyed, at the crowd outside the medical centre. Beatrix followed his gaze and saw with horror that Brown was pointing the pistol at Father Beltrano, who was standing with his arms outstretched. Brown looked crazed. The gunshot split the air like a clap of thunder. The priest's head jerked backwards, and he collapsed into the mud with a wet slap.

The crowd froze for several seconds and then erupted in panic. They scattered along the street, ducking into doors and alleyways as Brown's men fired into the air. Beatrix saw an elderly man pushed over and a child trampled in the crush. She heard a chilling wail as Sister Magda crawled across the ground to Father Beltrano. She cradled his head in her lap and wept as she made the sign of the cross over his body.

One of the guards took up position behind her and fired his pistol into the air, looking around him wildly, almost defiantly. Then, his eyes blazing, he lowered his arm and aimed down at the nun as she prayed over her fallen comrade.

31

Beatrix took aim with the AK-47. There would be no second chance. She squeezed off one round, and the slug struck the guard in the neck. He was dead before he hit the ground. The rest of Brown's men, realising they were under fire, scrambled for cover behind the Land Cruisers and in the alleyways.

"Francesco," Beatrix said, "get to your sister's house. I'll meet you there as soon as I can."

"You can't fight them all. I will stay and help you. I will—"

"Go now! Brown's men won't take prisoners. I've got enough to do here without worrying about you."

Francesco opened his mouth to protest, but then thought better of it. He turned and sprinted away without looking back. Beatrix turned her attention back to the street. The guards were still in their hiding places, trying to work out where the shot had come from.

She broke cover and started carefully along the street, sticking close to the walls. A guard in one of the vehicles saw her and started to clamber out, a rifle in his hand. Beatrix cut him down with a trio of shots to the chest.

She paused in a doorway and swept the rifle along the street. Dusk was settling, and the thick smoke from the blaze at the medical centre made it difficult to pick out the remaining locals from the guards.

A shadow moved to her left, and a second man emerged from the mouth of an alley. He dropped to one knee and fired. Two slugs slammed into the wooden door post above her head. Beatrix raked the alleyway with gunfire, and the guard slumped to the ground. She ran in a low crouch to an abandoned Cadillac and hunkered down behind the engine block, the only part of the vehicle that stood any real chance of stopping a high-calibre round.

She saw muzzle flash near the medical centre an instant before two more bullets clanged into the Cadillac's bodywork. She popped up from behind the engine, just long enough to return fire in two controlled bursts, and was rewarded with a scream from the shadows.

Another volley of shots punctured the metal, several of the rounds passing right through the car and punching out again close to where she was hiding. She pulled out the fresh magazine and reloaded before charging the weapon, rolling onto her stomach and sliding beneath the car. Two more shooters were running towards the Cadillac on opposite sides of the road, hoping to catch her in a crossfire. She raked a burst of gunfire at the nearest man, aiming for his knees. There was a shriek of pain as he went down.

She swung her aim back across the street, searching for the second man, but there was no sign of him, only shadows.

Controlling her breathing, she examined the doorways

and side alleys for any hint of movement that might give away her attacker.

Nothing.

Something small flew from the shadows and bounced off the hood of the Cadillac with a metallic clang. A dull grey object, the size of a cricket ball, dropped into the sand, barely two metres from where she lay.

Grenade.

She shoved herself out from under the car and leapt up, hurling herself across the hood.

The grenade exploded in a flash of heat and light, and the world spun before her eyes.

Shaking her head, trying to clear her senses, she saw that some of the oil drums outside the workshop had ignited, and the flames were taking a greedy hold of the tinder-dry shacks on both sides of the street.

Prosperidad was burning.

Her ears rang. Sounds came to her as though she were hearing them through wet felt. Someone was walking towards her, nearly silent in the aftermath of the explosion. She saw the combat boots and the rifle and the wide-brimmed hat.

It was Brown.

She looked around for a weapon. The AK lay in the mud, too far away.

She felt for the stiletto, but it was gone.

"Run out of luck, I see." Brown's voice was faint through the ringing in her ears.

He smiled as he raised the rifle to his shoulder and took aim.

She heard the gunshot.

But felt nothing.

Beatrix blinked.

Brown's mouth fell open in surprise. He took a step forward, staggering to keep his balance before he collapsed to his knees and fell face first into the mud.

Beatrix turned to see Sister Magda standing ten feet away, clutching a pistol in a two-handed grip.

32

Beatrix went to the nun and took the pistol.

"Sister Magda?" she said gently.

The nun did not respond. Her face was pale, and her eyes had the vacant stare of someone in shock.

Beatrix put an arm around her shoulders. "Come on. We need to go."

She supported Sister Magda's weight as they walked back along the deserted main street, past the bodies of the guards Beatrix had shot. Nothing broke the silence save for the crackling of the flames as the last timbers of the medical centre collapsed inwards, sending a shoal of sparks spiralling up into the night.

Sister Magda paused beside the body of Father Beltrano. She knelt down, pulled a clean square of linen from her pocket and laid it reverently over the man's face before saying a prayer and making the sign of the cross once more.

"I helped him to build this place," she said, getting to her feet again. "It was his life for ten years. He begged, borrowed and stole to get the equipment he needed. When he decided that the people needed something, he never rested until they had it." She looked around at the wreckage and the bodies littering the street. "He deserved better than this. Now it is up to me to finish his work."

"What do you want to do?"

"I have to go to my house. I have to collect his file and take it to Gomez in Guayana. He will help us to get the justice Father Jair was seeking."

Beatrix shook her head. "No. That would be suicide. That's where Rincon went. He'll know what happened here and have his thugs looking for you. You need to lie low."

Sister Magda's face was like carved stone. "You don't understand, Miss Archer. It's not up for debate. I have a responsibility to complete his work, and you have an obligation to help me."

"What?"

"I killed a man to save your life. And if *I* saved your life, that means *God* saved your life. You have a bargain to keep with Him. He brought you here for a purpose, whether you believe it or not."

There was little point arguing with the nun, Beatrix realised with grudging respect. The woman had a stubborn streak as wide as the Orinoco. Beatrix decided to humour her for now and try to dissuade her later. At least they were agreed on one thing: getting away from Prosperidad was the priority now.

She went over to one of the Land Cruisers; a man was slumped over the wheel. Checking that he was indeed dead, she dragged his body out the open door. It tumbled into the dirt with a heavy thud. She had counted seven dead guards in total, including Brown and the first man she had killed in the alleyway. She had no idea how many more might be creeping around here somewhere.

She found the keys still in the ignition. After helping

Sister Magda into the passenger seat, Beatrix climbed behind the wheel, gunned the engine and then followed Sister Magda's directions through the muddy lanes to the one-roomed shack that Beatrix had woken up in earlier that day. The poorest house, in the poorest part of a poor town.

Francesco raced out of the door to meet them. As the two women stepped out of the Land Cruiser, he enfolded his sister in a tight embrace.

"Thank the good Lord you're safe," she said, holding him at arm's length and looking him up and down. "I thought I'd never see you again."

"Helen came for me," said Francesco.

"She has been sent by God," Sister Magda said, giving Beatrix a pointed look.

Francesco turned to her. "Rincon's men are dead?"

"Yes, but he has others at the compound. He'll know what happened, and he won't take it lying down. He'll send more guards, and when they get here, they'll come looking for you and your sister. You both need to get away from here —preferably to somewhere that Rincon has no influence. Perhaps you can talk some sense into your sister about not going to Guayana."

Francesco raised his hands in submission. "I doubt it. Once her mind is made up, nothing can make her change it," he said.

"You should go with her, then."

"I can't. I understand the risks—I do. But my family is here. The families of my friends. If I run, then I will always be running from the next Rincon and the next Brown. You have given us hope, Señora Archer. Prosperidad belongs to us, and it is where I will make my stand with my friends and neighbours. My sister has her duty, and I have mine."

Beatrix took a deep breath and said nothing. Rincon's

pride would be bruised by what had happened tonight, and that would make him more dangerous and spiteful than ever. She had become involved in the fight against her better judgement, and now she was worried that she had condemned these people.

Sister Magda hurried into the shack now and emerged moments later carrying the large ring binder Beatrix had seen earlier and two plastic bottles of water.

Beatrix gave a weary sigh. "Forget about the file. It's just going to make you a bigger target for Rincon. Go somewhere safe, out of his reach."

Sister Magda raised her chin defiantly. "If you won't drive me to Guayana, then I will take one of the other trucks and drive myself. I am going—with or without you."

With that, the nun pushed past her and climbed back into the passenger seat of the Land Cruiser. She pulled the door shut and sat, staring straight ahead, holding the ring binder close to her chest.

Beatrix stared at her and then turned to Francesco. The man smiled sheepishly and then shrugged. "You know what she's like, Señora. Once she has made her mind up about something..."

"I'm beginning to get the idea."

33

They left Francesco at the front door of Sister Magda's shack as they rolled away into the darkness. Beatrix did not want to put on the high beams until they were clear of the town in case there were still some of Rincon's men around. They passed through the main street, where the ruined medical centre was now little more than a skeleton of blackened timber and glowing embers.

The bodies had all been moved from the street, as had the remaining Land Cruiser, though it was not clear who had done it. Beatrix guessed that Rincon's remaining contingent had come out to assess the damage and collect the bodies of their fallen comrades, and then headed back to the compound to wait for reinforcements. But she did not much want to put her theory to the test by dawdling. She put the Land Cruiser in gear and accelerated away from the town as soon as they were clear of the main street.

Driving through the forest at night was hard and tiring. The truck's beams penetrated no more than a hundred metres before they were lost in the gloom. The rough track was cratered with potholes filled with slimy brown water of indeterminable depth that Beatrix did not dare drive through. The journey would be perilous enough without getting stuck, particularly when Rincon's forces were more than likely already out hunting for them.

They drove in silence. Beatrix focused on the track ahead while Sister Magda held on grimly to her door handle, still clutching the ring binder to her chest. After an hour, they had travelled barely twenty miles. After three hours, the forest track widened, and the trees thinned out in favour of open scrubland and rolling hills. They turned onto a stony road that looked like a neglected farm track but felt like fresh blacktop after the muddy roller coaster of the forest.

The eastern sky was turning pale grey now, and Beatrix relaxed and sped up. She was in a lot of pain: her broken finger throbbed, the wound in her shoulder itched, and her eye socket still throbbed from the rifle blow. A stinging in the back of her thigh suggested that she might have picked up a sliver of shrapnel from the grenade.

Dawn broke, and she was relieved at finally being able to see the landscape again. The view was uninspiring, a wasteland of scrubby vegetation and solitary clumps of forest left behind by the loggers. At one point, they crossed a bridge over a sluggish brown river, and Beatrix spied haphazard settlements along the bank. They began to pass market stalls along the side of the road that sold fresh *arepas* and *mandocas* straight out of the fryer.

The warmth of the cabin began to get the better of Beatrix, and her eyelids grew heavy.

"Helen!"

She opened her eyes with a start to find the truck careering towards a ditch. She yanked the wheel straight.

"You need to take a break," Sister Magda said. "And we need food. There's a turn-off about five miles up the road. There's a place I know where we can get breakfast."

Beatrix did not argue. She *did* need a rest, and now that Sister Magda had mentioned food, she realised she had eaten nothing since the stew the nun had given her the previous day. She was ravenous.

She followed the directions to a small hamlet off the main route. The town was simple and unadorned: a dozen family homes of cinderblock with corrugated tin roofs, set in emerald-green fields of coffee and surrounded by jungle. A few of the homes were painted, but most were not; chickens strutted freely between the houses. They found a small cantina at the end of the town with a surprising number of dusty and battered cars in the parking lot.

"They only have six tables," Sister Magda said, "but they serve the best breakfast in Gran Sabana. People on their way to the city stop here every day."

Beatrix parked the truck and followed Sister Magda through the double doors to the cool interior of the building. The nun still clutched the file close to her chest, as though she was afraid it would vanish if she let it go. The inside of the cantina combined a dining room and general store. There were open sacks of beans by the door and tinned goods stacked neatly on shelves. Hungry diners crowded around plain, scrubbed wood tables and worked on large plates of food. The air was thick with steam and alive with rowdy conversation.

A woman in an apron emerged from the kitchen. She had black hair with an inch of grey at the roots. When she saw Sister Magda, she threw open her arms.

"Magdalena!" They embraced. "You don't come to see us

since you moved to the jungle. You are here to eat, yes? I won't let you leave until I have filled your belly."

Sister Magda's expression softened, and she laughed. "Thank you, Cordelia. You are so busy..."

"Nonsense, nonsense. I have the best table in the house for you, right over here."

Sister Magda's smile broadened, and Beatrix was struck at how attractive the nun was when she wasn't angry. She turned to Beatrix and extended her arm. "Cordelia—I would like you to meet Helen Archer. She is a friend from England who is taking me to Guayana."

Cordelia extended a hand, and Beatrix shook it. The woman then looked Beatrix up and down. "Perhaps you might like to freshen up a little before you eat. The bathroom is over there."

Beatrix could tell that it was not really a request, and, when she considered it, she realised how gritty and unpleasant she felt. She took her leave of the two women and found the small, spotless bathroom in the corner of the dining room. When she looked in the mirror, she realised exactly why Cordelia had made her suggestion. Her face was grubby with the red mud of Prosperidad, and her hair had crusted into something resembling dreadlocks. One side of her face was black with bruising, and the wound in her shoulder had reopened, and blood had seeped through her shirt. Her bandaged hand was filthy and swollen, and, as she had suspected earlier, there was a streak of fresh blood down the back of her leg from a small shrapnel wound.

She washed the filth from her face and hands, then rinsed the mud out of her hair as best she could. She had a fresh T-shirt in the backpack, and she changed into it quickly, stuffing the old shirt and her ruined jacket into the bathroom's trash can. She sponged the worst of the bloodstains from the rest of her clothes and looked again in the mirror.

It was an improvement. She still looked like she had been in a car accident, but, feeling a little refreshed, she returned to the dining room.

34

She found Sister Magda sitting at a table beneath an open window that overlooked the coffee fields. The ring binder lay beside her on a chair, and there were two glasses of juice on the table with fresh fruit floating in them. Beatrix's mouth began to water.

"I ordered for both of us. It's quicker that way."

"I don't care, as long as it's food."

"Try the *tisana*. They make it fresh every morning."

Beatrix picked up the glass and drank deeply. The juice was ice cold and sweet, and the fruit was delicious.

She put down the glass and looked around the dining room. Cordelia and a younger girl were serving a group at the next table.

"How do you know these people?" she said.

"From when I was a novice. I was posted here to teach in the school for a year." She indicated a young girl in an apron taking orders. "Back then, little Maria was barely walking. Look at her now!"

Beatrix looked at the girl and thought suddenly of Isabella. She looked away quickly and turned her attention back to Sister Magda, who looked happier than she ever had in Prosperidad. It was certainly a relief not to have to deal with her perpetual bad mood.

The nun caught Beatrix staring. "Is something wrong?"

Beatrix shook her head. "No. I'm fine."

Sister Magda sighed. "I should apologise," she said. "I've always had a fierce temper, even as a child. It has cost me many hours in the confessional over the years." She smiled sheepishly. "Father Jair used to say it would be my downfall."

"I'm sorry about your friend," said Beatrix truthfully. "And I never thanked you properly for saving my life. Where did you learn to handle a gun?"

Sister Magda smiled drily. "After I took my vows, I was given a posting to a church in the favelas of Caracas. One of the priests gave me a small pistol to carry when I went on outreach visits. It was useful to have it. The Lord God protects us from evil, but sometimes He needs a little extra help."

The food arrived. It was hot and plentiful and absolutely delicious: eggs, scrambled with fresh peppers, beans, fried plantains and freshly baked *arepas*, fluffy and still warm from the oven. Beatrix waited patiently while Sister Magda said grace over the meal, and then dived in. She ate quickly, tearing off chunks of *arepa* to scoop up the eggs and washing it all down with hot coffee that Maria and Cordelia refilled from an endless pot.

At last, Beatrix sat back and pushed her plate away. "I was hungry."

Sister Magda smiled and pushed back her own plate. She reached into the pocket of her dress and pulled out a packet of cigarettes and a lighter. She offered one to Beatrix, who accepted it, tucking it between her lips and leaning forward. Sister Magda lit them both and blew out a plume of blue smoke with a satisfied sigh.

"Can I ask you a question?"

"Sure," Beatrix said.

"Why do you do this? I mean—why do you work for the people you work for?"

Beatrix flicked ash into the ashtray. "I lost my daughter when she was little. She was taken from me by the people I used to work for. The only way I can get her back is by doing this." She waved her hand vaguely. "After I finish this job, I'm done. I want a quiet life."

Sister Magda nodded thoughtfully. "All of us have our own crosses to bear. I misjudged you, Helen. I'm sorry."

"Forget it," she said. "What now?"

"What do you mean?"

"What are we going to do now?"

"I'm going to go and deliver the evidence."

"You still want to do it?"

"What choice do I have?"

"I'm coming too," said Beatrix, surprising herself.

Sister Magda raised an eyebrow. "I thought you said you wouldn't. That you couldn't get involved."

"I've been thinking about that," she said carefully. "I'm here now. I'm involved."

"Is that it?" The nun narrowed her eyes at her, waiting. The woman was perceptive.

"No," said Beatrix. "There's more." She paused, searching for the right words. "The children in the medical centre... Seeing them was... hard for me. All I could think of was my daughter. Her name is Isabella." She looked at Sister Magda, who smiled.

"That is a very pretty name."

Beatrix nodded. "If she was ever that alone and helpless,

I'd want someone to be there for her, too." She stubbed out her cigarette. "Sorry—I don't know what I'm trying to say. Forget I said anything."

"It's the first thing you've said that makes sense." Sister Magda smiled again, more broadly this time. "And I'll be glad to have you with me."

Beatrix sat back and helped herself to another of Sister Magda's cigarettes. "Tell me about Gomez."

"He's a good man," said Sister Magda. "Father Jair met him when he was helping a group of people in the south to stop illegal loggers driving them off their land. He felt sure that Gomez would help us, too, if we brought him proof."

"We'll need to be careful," said Beatrix. "Rincon will know what happened in Prosperidad, and he has powerful friends. If he suspects anything, he'll have his people there waiting for us."

"I've thought of that. We will go to the convent where I trained as a novice. We'll be safe there."

35

The convent was in an unfashionable district near the river, away from the modern streets in the newer parts of the city. The houses and shops here were poor and the roads little more than hard-packed red dust. The convent was a low, red-brick building with a row of arches along the front and well-kept flowerbeds. Parked on the street directly in front of the convent was a blue and white Bolivar State police car.

Beatrix and Sister Magda sat in the Land Cruiser in the shadows of a narrow lane across the street. They had been watching the car for ten minutes. The nun's ring binder sat between her feet in the footwell now, neatly tucked into a shopping bag.

"It's probably just coincidence," said Sister Magda. "There's a lot of crime in this area. They might be talking to the nuns to find out if they've seen anything suspicious. It happened all the time when I lived here."

Beatrix shook her head. "I don't believe in coincidences. And impatience is a good way to get yourself killed. We came here because you said it was safe, and now we find the police parked right outside—it doesn't feel right."

Sister Magda let out an exasperated sigh. "You're just being paranoid."

She started to get out of the car, but Beatrix placed a restraining hand on her arm. "Humour me. Wait here a minute while I check it out."

Sister Magda rolled her eyes, but stayed where she was. Beatrix put on a pair of mirrored sunglasses she had found in the glove box, then walked casually across the road to the empty police car. She glanced up and down the road and then tried the door handle. It was locked. There was a clipboard on the passenger seat with smudgy printouts from the day's despatches. Beatrix took another look along the road, then picked up a rock and smashed it hard against the passenger-side window. The toughened glass burst inwards. Beatrix reached in and grabbed the clipboard and then hurried back across the road to the Land Cruiser.

She got back into the car and rifled through the sheaf of paper. "Street robberies and drug deals, mostly. And a currency dealer was shot dead about three streets from here."

"That's more or less normal for this part of town. Are you satisfied now? Can we go in? I need to wash some of this grime off my face."

"Wait. Look at this."

She pulled out a sheet about midway down the pile. At the top of the page were two grainy, high-contrast photographs of herself and Sister Magda. She handed the sheet to the nun.

Sister Magda took it and scanned down the page. She blanched, and her hand went to her mouth. "It says we're wanted for burning down the hospital in Prosperidad. It says five children were killed in the blaze. Dear Lord—what have they done?" She handed the paper back to Beatrix, looking frightened now.

Beatrix scowled. "It's Rincon. He's guessed what we're doing and planted a story about us. They'll be watching anywhere they think we might go." She thought for a moment. "Does Rincon know about Gomez and what you and Father Jair planned to do? Think carefully."

Sister Magda swallowed and shook her head. "No, I don't see how he could," she said. "Father Jair never told anyone about Julian. I was the only one who knew."

"Good." Beatrix clipped the loose page back onto the clipboard, tossed it into the back of the car and then started the engine. "In that case we'll go straight to him."

36

Rincon paced angrily back and forth across the tarmac. Rodrigo Ferdinand leaned against a wall in the shade of the airport building, sucking on a thin cheroot.

"Calm down," Ferdinand said. "You give me hypertension just looking at you."

"Imbeciles and cretins," spat Rincon. "I gave that moron one simple task. *One!* Get that woman to tell us what she knows, then shoot her in the head and be done with it. How could he have fucked that up?"

"You can ask him yourself," said Ferdinand, taking a long drag from the cheroot. "Look."

He pointed away across the concrete apron where the black silhouette of the executive helicopter had just appeared above the tree line. The two men fixed their gaze on the black speck until it swooped in to land on the helipad. Rincon clenched and unclenched his fists as the rotors wound down with a whining sound. The pilot opened the door and unfolded the short flight of steps; then Vincente Bello stepped down onto the asphalt.

Rincon had heard what had happened to him: the woman had stabbed him in the eye with a hypodermic. Given that, he looked calm. He was dressed in black, as usual, with a patch over his injured eye. His face was cold as he crossed the tarmac towards them.

"Well?" Rincon said. "What have you got to say for yourself? I paid for the best, and this is what I get?"

Bello's expression did not change. "I do not take kindly to insults, Señor Rincon. Even from you."

"I paid you to get rid of that woman. Now half of my men are dead, including my head of security, while she is still out there doing God knows what."

"I will still take care of it. That is why I am here. As for your men? They were incompetent. They brought it on themselves."

Rincon wanted to rage at him, but held his tongue. "What now, then? How will you fix this?"

"Archer left Prosperidad in the company of a nun from the village—Sister Magdalena Constanza."

"We know that," said Ferdinand. "I have some influence with the chief of state police. They have a warrant out for the arrest of both women. If they're here, they'll find them."

"They *are* here. But I am not convinced that the police will find them. Archer is a professional—I suspect she has been trained by one of the European intelligence agencies. She will know how to make herself invisible."

"So?" Rincon said. "How are you going to find her?"

"My networks are different from those of the police. I will find them."

Rincon shook his head. "What if it's too late? I need to know how much she knows about the gold mine. And I need to know what she's doing here in Guayana. I can't risk any more interference. We are at a delicate stage in the proposal."

Bello nodded. "After the women left Prosperidad, I searched the house belonging to the nun. I found correspondence between Father Jair Beltrano and various environmental groups. He was trying to have charges brought against your mine, Señor Rincon. I suspect the nun is here about that. She is continuing his campaign to have you closed down."

Rincon ran his hands through his hair. "This could destroy everything. If the plans for the mine are made public, I'll go to jail. You will, too," he said, looking sharply at Ferdinand. He glanced over at the helicopter still cooling on the landing pad. "Maybe I should just go back to the compound. I could hide out there until this matter is dealt with."

"Not wise," said Bello. "As I said—your security is poor, and several of your men have been killed. And the people of Prosperidad are angry about what happened to the priest. You won't be safe there now."

"Well, what do you want me to do? Just *sit* here?"

Ferdinand put his hand on Rincon's shoulder. "That's *exactly* what you should do. Señor Bello—you say you can find her?"

"I believe so."

"Good," Ferdinand said. He turned back to Rincon. "So, you let him get on with the job while we focus on what *we* have to do. I've spoken to my friends in the militia. They have arranged for a squad to be placed on manoeuvres in Prosperidad for the next three weeks. They will keep the peace until you can replace your own security staff. They will be there in the next three or four days. All you have to do is wait here until then. You just need to relax."

"Easy for you to say," Rincon said.

"I know. But it's true. Tomorrow, I will host a dinner in your honour at my mansion. You will be recognised for your services to environmentalism, and I will formally sign the contract giving you licence to expand your operations across the Orinoco Mining Arc. The deal will make us rich, my friend. So, please—don't ruin it with impatience."

"Fine," Rincon conceded. "I'll stay. But I am making you responsible for my safety." He wagged a finger in Ferdinand's face, then turned to Bello. "As for you, just do your job properly this time."

37

The address was in the poorest part of town, one of three red blocks parked on a grimy plot of land between the main interstate and the goods yards. Packs of stray dogs roamed the hard-packed earth around the apartment buildings, and rubbish blew across the open ground.

"Tough neighbourhood," said Beatrix as they stepped out of the car.

"Not so bad," Sister Magda said. "The people here have water and electricity most days of the week, and the murder rate is lower than it is in Caracas. It might not look it, but this is actually a desirable area—at least, by comparison."

They found the right building, and Beatrix parked the Land Cruiser as close to the entrance as she could, wondering ruefully if it would still be there when they returned. Sister Magda climbed out, hefting the bag holding the ring binder, and the two women set off along the cracked front walkway and began to make their way up a concrete stairwell that smelled of urine. Beatrix rounded a bend in the stairs and stopped. Four boys in hooded sweatshirts were gathered on the landing above, smoking a joint. When they saw Beatrix, they closed ranks, their faces hardening.

The smallest boy stepped forward and spat on the stairs in front of her. *"Que quieres, perra?"*

Sister Magda pushed past her on the stairs before she could reply. She stepped up to the boy, and, even though she was a full head shorter, she wagged a finger in his face and unleashed a torrent of Spanish. Beatrix heard what she thought were colourful expletives. The boys backed away, apologised, then squeezed past them and headed downstairs, their eyes averted from the two women. Two of them made the sign of the cross as they passed.

"That was unexpected." Beatrix gave Sister Magda a wry smile. "What did you say to them?"

"They're not afraid of me," she said. "But the fear of God is strong in the poor. They know they might be meeting Him sooner than they'd like."

Julian Gomez's apartment was on the top floor, about halfway along an open breezeway that looked down onto the street below. There was no bell, so Beatrix rapped on the flimsy door with her knuckles. There was a long delay before a voice called from inside.

"Who is it?"

"Señor Gomez, it's Sister Magda. From Prosperidad. I'm a friend of Father Beltrano's."

A security chain rattled, and the door opened a few inches. "And your friend?"

"Also a friend," said Sister Magda. "Please—let us in, Señor Gomez. We've come a long way to ask for your help."

The man behind the door regarded them suspiciously for a few seconds; then the door closed before reopening fully. The man in the doorway was lean and dressed in a pale linen suit and sky-blue shirt. The jacket's sleeves were rolled up to his elbows. A knitted tie was undone at his neck. A pair of horn-rimmed spectacles and floppy black hair completed the impression of a young academic who had just been woken from a nap on the sofa.

"I don't understand," he said. "Where is Father Beltrano? His last letter was six months ago. He said he was coming to see me, then... nothing."

"We can explain," said Sister Magda. "Perhaps we could come in?"

"I don't know you." Gomez looked nervous. "I was expecting Father Beltrano, not you. I think you should—"

"Father Beltrano is dead," said Beatrix. "Aurelio Rincon's men murdered him last night."

Gomez blinked at Beatrix. "Dead?"

"There was no way to let you know before we came here," said Beatrix. "But we've brought the evidence that Father Beltrano was compiling."

Gomez blinked again. "Evidence? What evidence?"

"The evidence that Father Jair was collecting about the mine," said Sister Magda. She fished in the shopping bag and pulled out the ring binder. "It's all here. Assay reports, photographs, eyewitness accounts. He said there was enough evidence here for you to close down the mine."

Julian Gomez was looking close to panic. He backed away. "No," he muttered. "I can't accept that. I can't get involved. You need to leave now."

"I'm sorry," Sister Magda said. "I don't understand. Father Jair said you'd agreed to help. He said you were an honest man who would help bring Aurelio Rincon to justice for what he has done."

"That was before," blurted Gomez.

"Before *what*?"

"Things have changed. You have to leave." He placed his hand on the edge of the door and made to close it.

"We *can't* leave," Sister Magda insisted, stepping forward and stopping the door with her foot. "You're the last hope we have. You have to—"

"Out!"

There was a small telephone table in the hallway. Gomez turned and rummaged in the drawer and came up holding an old, heavy-looking revolver. He held it shakily in two hands, staring wildly from the nun to Beatrix and back again.

Beatrix crossed the short distance and slapped the gun out of his hands. She grabbed his collar and swept his legs, dropping him heavily onto the floor.

He tried to scramble away. "Please," he begged. "Please don't kill me."

"What are you talking about?" Sister Magda said.

Beatrix picked up the pistol, tucked it into her waistband and pulled Gomez up by the arm. "We're not going to kill you," she said. "Pull yourself together and get up before I lose my temper."

Gomez did, and allowed himself to be led into the small living room. Sister Magda closed the door and hurried to join them. There was a large dark wood desk, heavily scarred from years of use and piled with stacks of papers and magazines. The walls were lined with well-thumbed books—political writings and biographies—and there were revolutionary portraits and posters on the walls. Beatrix thought that it looked like an undergraduate's bedsitting room. A pile of unwashed dinner plates on the floor beside the chair completed the picture of a man who lived alone and either didn't care about personal hygiene or was too busy to notice the state into which he had allowed his rooms to fall.

Gomez slumped into the desk chair and took off his glasses. "I'm sorry," he said without looking at either of them. "About the gun. Things have become so dangerous here, and then when you told me that Father Jair... I panicked."

"Why is it dangerous?" Beatrix said. "What's happened?"

"The mining consortia that operate in the Orinoco Mining Arc—they're gangsters. They don't care about anything other than making as much money as they can. The environment? Human rights? Those mean nothing to them."

"We know that," Sister Magda said. "We've just come from Prosperidad."

"It's the same all over the Gran Sabana. The government takes bribes to grant the licences, and they don't care what happens after that. The jungles are hundreds of miles away. Out of sight, out of mind."

"But you can help us? Father Jair said you were an honest politician and that you'd helped others."

Gomez bit his lip. "I *have* done," he said. "I have friends, a few dedicated activists and lawyers who have helped me to make the case for others in the past. But the gangs know. There have been murders. Politicians have been assassinated. Only last week one of my lawyers was shot outside his office." He shook his head grimly. "And now you come and tell me that Father Jair has been murdered. I don't think I can help you, Señora. Things have become too dangerous in Ciudad Guayana."

Sister Magda stared at him helplessly.

"We came a long way to find you," Beatrix said, taking over. "Father Jair had faith in you. He died trying to put together the evidence that you would need. The least you can do is read it."

Gomez looked away, bit his lip, then looked back at Beatrix again. "You're right. I should—I will."

"And then?"

"I don't know. If it looks like there's a case? Maybe. But I promise nothing. I have to think of myself. My wife and daughter are in Caracas. I have to think of them."

"Of course," said Sister Magda. "And thank you. We will gladly take whatever help you can give us."

Gomez wiped his mouth with the back of his hand. "I need a coffee and a cigarette. I'm afraid I have nothing in the house, but there is a café around the corner. We could go there while I read the file."

38

T he café was five minutes' walk away. Sister Magda took the opportunity to tell Gomez what had happened to Father Beltrano.

"*Madre de Dios*," he muttered. "These animals are out of control. That they would do such a thing to a priest is beyond contempt. There is no one they would not kill or bribe. Half the judiciary in Bolivar State are on their payroll."

The café was sparse, laid out simply with wooden chairs and tables covered with plastic. They were served by an engaging young man named Raoul who greeted Gomez by name and brought them three cups of fresh, hot coffee as rich as dark chocolate. Gomez settled into a chair facing the door and lit a cigarette before he opened the file. Sister Magda and Beatrix sat opposite and said nothing while he sipped his drink and flicked through the pages.

He read for five minutes and then shook his head in disbelief. "This is *outrageous*. Father Jair has documented the symptoms of mercury poisoning in more than eighty children. There are reports of child labour, accidents and deaths. And the assay reports seem to prove conclusively that the mine is poisoning the water courses."

Sister Magda leaned across the table. "Then there is enough to convict Rincon?"

"Enough to bring a persuasive case. But that is not the problem."

"What is?" said Beatrix.

"Rincon is the problem," said Gomez. "Or, rather, his business partner. The rumour is that Rodrigo Ferdinand has an interest in the gold mine."

"And he is?"

"A government minister—and untouchable. We'd need very strong evidence to convict Rincon. Something that couldn't be denied or argued around by a clever lawyer. This material is good, but I don't know if it is good enough."

"This isn't all that Rincon is doing," said Beatrix. "He's planning to open up a new gold seam at the top of the mountain. He's going to blow away the cliff face overlooking the town so he can get to the gold and make it look like an accident. He doesn't care who gets killed in the process."

Gomez's eyes widened. "You can prove this?"

"I overheard him telling Ferdinand," said Beatrix. "And I found boreholes and explosives. The mountain is already rigged to blow. If I can get back there and take some photographs, I can prove it."

"That would certainly be enough," Gomez said. "It would be undeniable—even a paid judge wouldn't dare to contradict it publicly."

"Then you'll help us?" said Sister Magda.

Gomez shut the file with a snap. "I need to consult with some colleagues. I'll talk to the lawyers I know and see what they think. If—and *only* if—they agree, then I'll start preparing a case."

Sister Magda clapped her hands. "Praise the Lord. Thank you, Señor Gomez. I knew Father Jair was right about you."

"But you must be careful. If Rincon hears of what we are proposing, they will send killers after us. You shouldn't stay in a hotel—they'll watch them. You can stay in my apartment for now. It's nothing special, but at least you'll be safe."

"What else would be useful for you?" Beatrix asked.

Gomez thought for a moment. "It would be good to know what Rincon is doing in Guyana. If he is in business with Ferdinand and we can prove it, that would also help our case." He looked at Beatrix. "Can you see what you can find out about his business here? We used to have a private detective who did that sort of work, but he was murdered last year."

"I'll see what I can find."

Gomez looked at her dubiously. "I don't know," he said. "Perhaps it would be better if I asked someone else?"

Beatrix smiled. "I can handle it."

Gomez tucked the file under his arm, paid for the coffees and led the way to the door.

RAOUL WATCHED THEM GO. He waited in the doorway, watching until they disappeared around the corner of the street before going to the back of the café and pulling his cellphone out of his pocket. He typed in a number, then tapped his foot nervously while he waited to be connected.

"Hello? It's Raoul—from the café. You were right—he came in with two women. They look like the ones you described—one old, the other younger. They left about three minutes ago." He paused and licked his lips. "That's what you wanted—right? I'll get my money?" He glanced anxiously over his shoulder. "Remember it was Raoul who told you. Make sure the message gets to Señor Bello."

39

Back at Gomez's apartment block, Beatrix waited outside while Gomez and Sister Magda went up to the flat. She pulled her phone out of the backpack and dialled Michael Yeung's number in Hong Kong, looking around while she waited for a connection. The boys they had seen in the stairwell earlier were lounging outside the building, but they did not seem inclined to bother her.

"Beatrix," Michael said, "is the job done?"

"As good as."

"What does that mean? Is he dead or not?"

"Not yet. But the evidence about what he's been doing has been passed to the authorities. He's going to get investigated, and then he's going to jail. There's nothing else I can do here."

There was a pause. She knew from long experience that it was Michael's way of giving her time to reflect on what she had just said.

"That wasn't what you were told to do," he said eventually. "I didn't send you to *disgrace* Rincon; I sent you to *kill* him. Rincon is connected. He will shrug off any investigations against him. He needs to die. He betrayed me—that is the consequence. It will send a message to my enemies."

Beatrix took a deep breath and tried another tack. "His influence extends high up in government. I told you—he's connected with the Minister for Mining."

"Rodrigo Ferdinand. I know."

"Rincon is under his protection—I'm not sure how I'll be able to get to him."

"That doesn't sound like you."

"The risks are too high, and his days are numbered whatever I do. The situation will resolve itself if you just leave it alone. I just want to get out of here and see Isabella. Couldn't you just—"

"No. We have a contract. You do as I ask and I'll tell you where to find Isabella. No other arrangement is acceptable."

"What do you expect me to do? You want me to hunt down Rincon and Ferdinand? I don't even know where to start looking."

"I can help you with that. I looked into Ferdinand. He has made a lot of money for himself through his underworld connections—and some of those people don't like him very much. It didn't take much to win them to our side. Ferdinand is hosting a dinner at his mansion to give out environmental awards to all of his closest associates in the mining cartels. The most prestigious award of the evening will be presented to Rincon."

"When is this?"

"Tomorrow."

"And you want me to kill him there, in front of his guests and surrounded by his security, to send a message that no one messes with you?"

"Let me give you the address."

40

The minister's mansion was one of a dozen large properties overlooking the river near the old town of San Felix. The Orinoco did not make the most picturesque of backdrops; it was a broad, muddy ribbon that was heavily congested with freight shipping. But the pillars and porticos of the house, built in the traditional English style and set among sumptuous gardens, went some way towards imparting a sense of elegance.

Beatrix and Sister Magda sat in Gomez's cramped Renault and watched a succession of vehicles enter and leave through the main gates a hundred metres away. It had been Gomez's idea that they should take his car when Beatrix had laid out her plan to stake out Ferdinand's property. Beatrix would have suggested it in any event; their own car would almost certainly be on the police watchlist and was not worth the risk of using anymore.

Beatrix knew the preparations for the party presented an opportunity to sneak inside and have a look around, but she also knew that an event of this magnitude of importance would have security to match. At least six catering vans had entered the premises; several of them had parked up by the gates, waiting their turn to approach the house and unload their cargo. That suggested a guest list that might number in the hundreds.

Sister Magda shifted in her seat. "What are you going to do?"

"I have to get inside," she said. "I need a proper look around."

The two women looked up as a long Mercedes limousine swept out of the gate and rolled past them. Beatrix had a clear view of Rincon and Ferdinand in the back seat; both men were lost in conversation. She watched as the car disappeared into the distance.

"How would you get inside? They're stopping everyone."

Beatrix scanned the high walls that ran around the property. "If I wait until dark, I could go over the wall and hide in the grounds until the party starts."

Sister Magda thought for a moment, looking out the window of the car. Suddenly her face brightened. "I know an easier way."

"What?"

"Dress as one of the catering staff. You could go anywhere you wanted."

Beatrix smiled patiently. "We'd need someone on the inside with a uniform and a security pass. I don't suppose you can suggest anyone?"

"Maybe I can," said Sister Magda. "Follow me."

The nun was out of the car and striding up the road before Beatrix could stop her. She made her way to one of the catering trucks that had parked by the main gates. A young man in chef's whites was leaning against the side of the van with a hand-rolled cigarette in his mouth.

"Ricky!" Sister Magda said. "I knew it was you."

The young man's eyes opened, and he gaped as if he had just seen a ghost. "Sister Magda?"

"Still smoking that ungodly weed?"

The young man glanced down at the joint in his hand as though he hadn't realised it was there, then quickly tossed it on the ground and stamped it out. "I'm sorry. I didn't—"

"I might have known you wouldn't have mended your ways. It was the same in the seminary—always running off, smoking and drinking and chasing girls when you should've been practising your catechism and studying for your exams. I always said you would come to no good."

She drove home each sentence by jabbing her forefinger into the young man's chest, then stepped back and tutted at him, folding her arms.

"Sister Magda—look! I'm working. I have a good job as a waiter for a catering firm—see?" He turned and indicated the logo on the side of the van, then smiled hopefully.

Sister Magda glared at him suspiciously. "And what about the drugs?"

"That was a mistake," he said, holding up his hands. "Just the one. Never again."

Sister Magda turned to Beatrix. "There was an incident in Ricky's final year when he was found smoking something that he shouldn't have been smoking. I stood up for him when everyone else had decided that he ought to be expelled. Isn't that right, Ricky?"

"Yes," he said sheepishly. "And I've always been grateful. I would never have got this job if I'd been expelled. I'd have ended up hanging around with the gangs. Things would not have gone so well for me."

"It's just as well we met again, then, isn't it? If only to remind you of what you stand to lose." She looked at the van. "It is a good job?"

The young man nodded vigorously. "Very good. They trained me to serve at the tables, and I get to do all the big events in Guayana. I know I owe it to you, Sister. If there's anything I can ever do for you, you only need ask."

Sister Magda smiled. "There is something you can do, as it happens. I'd like you to meet my friend Helen."

41

The flat was in darkness. It was silent save for the ticking of a small clock on the mantelpiece. The metallic snick of the front door latch being slipped echoed in the hallway, and the door creaked open just enough to allow Bello to slip inside. He paused just inside the door, listening for anything that suggested that someone was home, but there was nothing. He smiled. That was good; it made his work easier.

Bello moved into the living room. His gaze alighted on the desk. A ring binder lay open on it, spilling out photographs and other documents. He pulled out his cellphone and turned on the flashlight, then flipped quickly through the documents. One report caught his eye, and he picked it up and read it quickly. It was an eyewitness statement from Prosperidad. Rincon had been right: Archer and the nun *were* trying to make a case against him.

He checked the other rooms. Three used coffee cups in the kitchen, along with the binder, heightened his suspicions that the two women were staying at the flat with

Gomez. That was good. With luck, he could take care of this whole thing tonight.

Bello returned to the study. He set down his attaché case and flipped the catches, removing what looked like a thick block of putty that was wrapped in plastic and bound with insulating tape. He took his time, fixing the packet to the underside of the desk and taking care to make sure it was out of sight. When he was satisfied, he completed the assembly process; he inserted the small detonator and ran the wire out to the side of the desk.

Bello pondered. He could wire the detonator to a timer that was set to go off in the early hours when they would all be in the flat together. But that was haphazard. He was better than that. He liked to be sure.

Then he saw it: the wire trailing from the desk lamp to a small plastic switch. He wound the detonation wire into the lamp's braided cable so that it wouldn't be visible. He took out a small optician's screwdriver and removed the back of the switch, twisting the exposed ends of the detonator into the terminals. He reassembled the switch and closed the attaché case.

Bello took a last look around to make sure nothing had been disturbed and then slipped out the way he had come.

B eatrix kept her head down as she helped push the heavy catering trolley past the gatehouse. Ricky Torres was on the other end of the trolley. He waved and smiled to the guards as they trundled past.

"Crockery and place settings," he shouted cheerily, pointing to the trolley.

"Go through."

The black and white uniform Ricky had found for Beatrix in the back of his van was about three sizes too large, and she had had to secure loose folds of material with the bulldog clip that Ricky used to secure his requisition forms. It wasn't comfortable, and she knew she wouldn't pass muster if anyone looked too carefully, but it seemed that she had made it through the first line of security.

She looked up at the house. The mansion featured a portico and Doric columns along the white painted frontage and double bay windows on either side of the large front doors. A metal ramp had been laid across the front steps to allow the steady stream of catering staff to wheel trolleys into the house.

"How many people are you catering for?" Beatrix asked quietly as they trundled the trolley up the ramp.

"Two hundred," said Ricky. "We do all the big parties in Ciudad Guayana, and this is one of the largest I've seen. Señor Ferdinand is a big man in this town." He swallowed. "I could get in a lot of trouble for this."

"Don't worry. I told you—I just want to look around."

Ricky nodded uneasily. Sister Magda had told him that Beatrix was a freelance journalist preparing a piece on Rodrigo Ferdinand. She had explained that Ferdinand had rebuffed Beatrix's request to visit him, so she was getting material for her article in other ways.

"What about the money?" he whispered.

"One hundred dollars cash as soon as we're done. Promise. Now—can we get going?"

He nodded. "Just follow me. And if anyone asks—"

"My name is Dolores. Don't worry—I remember."

Besides the uniform, Ricky had given her a security pass that was laminated with the name Dolores Baptiste. Dolores's photograph showed a woman who was black and about two hundred and fifty pounds. It wasn't, Beatrix had concluded, the most carefully designed cover she had ever had, but needs must.

They passed through the main entrance and wheeled the trolley across the black and white marbled flooring of the vast entrance hall. A staircase swept up to the first floor. To their right, a set of double doors opened into a large ballroom.

Ricky led them quickly across the hallway and into the kitchens, a restaurant-sized affair with stainless-steel counters and red tiled floors. More staff unloaded trolleys and stacked crockery and glassware, while half a dozen chefs took stock of ingredients and started to prepare for the banquet. Beatrix glanced back at the doors. There was not much more she could learn by standing in the kitchen.

"I'm going to take a look around," she said.

Beatrix left before he could complain. She grabbed a clipboard from one of the kitchen counters on the way out and paused in the hallway, pretending to consult a list while she scanned the area. She noted the staircase to the upper floors and the two security guards lounging at the bottom. They looked relaxed and uncaring.

She stepped into the ballroom. A road crew was erecting a temporary stage and a lighting rig at one end of the hall, while about a dozen staff assembled round dining tables of the sort rented out by events firms. Dining chairs uphol-stered in red velvet were stacked along one wall.

Ferdinand was pushing the boat out.

She went back into the entrance hall. One of the guards had disappeared, and the other was engaged in conversation with someone who looked like the maître d' of an expensive restaurant. Beatrix caught a few words as she passed.

"We *cannot* have the guests seeing men with guns. Stay out of the way when people arrive."

"Take it up with the boss," the guard said. "Ferdinand said he wanted us visible at all times. He's got another squad patrolling outside—get used to it."

That was bad news. Ferdinand wasn't taking any risks, even in his own house. She wondered if she shouldn't abandon the plan altogether and go after Rincon in another location. But she knew that was a hopeless idea. As soon as he left here, Rincon would most likely fly straight back to his compound, and that would make him even harder to reach.

It was here or nowhere.

She saw a closed doorway on the other side of the hall.

No one had entered or left through it, which suggested that it was probably an area that was off-limits—and therefore of interest. While the guard was preoccupied, she crossed the hallway and tried the door. It was unlocked; she slipped inside.

She found herself in a large study furnished in dark wood and leather. Every available metre of wall space was lined with shelves holding identically bound books of equal height, each one carefully aligned with its neighbour. Their crisp spines told her that none of them had ever been opened. She crossed to a wooden desk the size of a small family car and tried the drawers. She found stationery, pencils, envelopes, a bottle of ink and paperclips. There was a Guayana phone directory and a bottle of indigestion tablets. There was nothing relating to Ferdinand's business or his associates.

She paused and looked around the room. The space had the appearance of having been designed as a showcase; somewhere for Ferdinand to hold video conferences surrounded by the trappings of power. She spent a few minutes searching the bookshelves to see if any of the leather volumes concealed a safe or a latch that would open a secret room, but there was nothing.

She let herself out into the hallway again and then froze where she stood. Ferdinand and Rincon were coming out of the ballroom. Rincon's face looked like thunder.

"*Relax*," Ferdinand was saying. "I've doubled the security for the dinner tomorrow. No one gets in without being checked."

"All right," Rincon said dubiously. "But I told you—she's dangerous. Do you know how many of my men I've lost because of her?"

The two men were too deep in their conversation to

notice her. She ducked behind a large vase of cut flowers on a plinth at the bottom of the stairs and pretended to study her clipboard. Ferdinand appeared unruffled, but Rincon was much more agitated than when she had last seen him. He fidgeted, and his eyes were wide and intense. Out of the corner of her eye, she noticed flecks of a white powder on his upper lip, and the reason for his agitation suddenly became clear: Rincon had a cocaine habit.

The two men paused at the bottom of the stairs. "You worry too much," Ferdinand said. "She's not going to cause us a problem. And Bello is on the case. This time tomorrow your problems will be over and we will be on the way to making our fortunes."

Rincon was not to be placated. "You need to take this more seriously. You need to take proper care of me if you expect to see a cent out of my gold mine."

Beatrix decided that she had heard enough. She stepped away from the vase of flowers and headed back to the kitchen.

B y the time Beatrix and Sister Magda returned to Gomez's apartment block, darkness had settled on the city, and the few streetlamps cast dim pools of light across the street. Sister Magda smiled as they climbed out of Gomez's Renault.

"How much did you give him?"

"A hundred and fifty," said Beatrix.

"He'll just spend it on more weed."

"He's young. I can think of worse things to spend it on."

"We agreed a hundred."

"The extra is an investment. He said he could get me back inside at any time."

Sister Magda frowned. "You're going back?"

Beatrix shrugged. "Maybe. It depends on what Julian comes up with."

"Hey! Wait!"

"Speak of the devil," Beatrix said.

They both turned to see Julian Gomez unfolding himself from a taxi a little way down the street. He paid the driver and hurried towards them. He carried his briefcase in one hand and a bottle wrapped in tissue paper in the other. He wore a huge grin and looked very different from the frightened man they had met the day before.

"How did you get on?" he said. "Find anything useful?"

Beatrix shrugged. "A few snippets. Ferdinand's planning a party tomorrow, and Rincon is the guest of honour. I might go back and see what else I can find out."

Gomez's grin widened. "You may not have to do that after the day I've had."

"Why?"

Gomez fell into step between the two women. "I went to see a lawyer who I've worked with before. A good guy, a true socialist, not like the pigs in government who are just out for what they can get." He held up the briefcase. "I showed him some of the highlights from the evidence. He said he'd never seen anything like it."

"Meaning?" Beatrix said.

"He thinks we've got a really strong case."

"Really?" Sister Magda's eyes glittered. "That's wonderful."

"Of course, there's a long way to go, and we still have a lot of work to do. But, still... I don't know how many times the two of you have instructed lawyers, but, in my experience, they tend to be pessimistic when thinking about new instructions. And he wasn't. He's confident that we have plenty to be working with."

Beatrix nodded. "Good job."

She knew, though, that this might make things more difficult for her. If Gomez's lawyer friend thought there was the prospect of a successful prosecution, there would be less incentive for her to return to the house. Why would they need any additional evidence? She kept her face carefully neutral; she would deal with that when she had to.

"I was thinking we should celebrate," Gomez said. He held up the bottle. "This is a very nice Chilean wine, made by a friend of mine who emigrated a couple of years ago. I thought we could have a drink to celebrate, then go to a nice little restaurant I know not far from here. Real country cooking and not too expensive."

Beatrix was silent for a moment, thinking. If Gomez was confident that a case could be made against the mine, then there really wasn't any further need for her to stay on here with him and Sister Magda. She could celebrate with the two of them tonight, then leave in the morning, happy in the knowledge that she had done all she could to help. She would still have to deal with Rincon in order to satisfy Michael, but it would be easier if she was alone.

Sister Magda patted her pockets as they reached the front door. "Bother," she muttered. "I left my cigarettes in the car."

Beatrix sensed her opportunity to talk to Sister Magda alone for a few minutes. "I'll come with you," she said.

Gomez went inside, and Beatrix followed Sister Magda back down to the car.

The nun opened the passenger door and reached into the glove box.

"I've been thinking," Beatrix said. "You don't need me anymore."

Sister Magda straightened and looked at her with concern. "You're not thinking of leaving?"

"It's time. I need to find my daughter. I'll leave first thing in the morning."

The nun frowned. "But you said you'd help us."

"I did. Julian has the evidence. What comes next is up to him. There's nothing more for me—"

The explosion cut her off in mid-sentence.

They felt the blast before they heard it. A wave of pressure moving at a thousand feet per second slammed into them, throwing them both to the ground. Then came the explosion, a wash of heat and a noise so loud that it overwhelmed the senses. Bricks and rubble rained onto the pavement.

Beatrix looked up. The windows of Gomez's flat had been reduced to blackened holes, belching flame and oily black smoke. The front door had gone, and the balcony railings were twisted and hanging from their supports.

"Julian!"

Sister Magda had a cut on her forehead, and blood was running down her face. She clambered awkwardly to her feet and began to stagger across the road towards the apartment block. Beatrix caught her by the arm.

"Let me go! I have to help him. He might be injured. He'll be—"

"He's dead," Beatrix said. "You can't help him now."

Doors were opening along the breezeway, and men and women were fleeing for the stairwells.

"What do we do?" Sister Magda cried. "What do we do?"

Beatrix looked up and down the road. People were gathering on the street and pointing up at the burning flat. In the distance she heard the sound of a siren.

"We need to leave," she said quickly, taking Sister Magda's arm. "Away from here, as quickly as possible. Whoever did this might still be around."

She led the dazed woman away down the street at a brisk walk. They had scarcely gone a dozen paces when a powerful engine rumbled into life at the mouth of a side street. A pair of headlights came on, pinning them in the beams.

A pickup truck accelerated hard towards them.

Beatrix hurled herself against the nun, knocking her sideways as the vehicle mounted the pavement where they had been standing only a moment before. The rear end fish-tailed wildly as the truck regained the road and roared away into the darkness, but not before Beatrix had a clear view of the man at the wheel.

It was Bello, the tidy little man who had interrogated her at the compound.

44

B eatrix took the car keys from Sister Magda, telling her to sit tight, and brushed aside the nun's protests before racing back to the Renault. She started the car, swung it through a U-turn and then accelerated hard after Bello. She turned into the dense flow of Saturday night traffic at the end of the street and headed towards downtown.

She spotted the large pickup up ahead. The Renault's engine was no match for the truck's power in a straight chase, but Bello had not yet realised he was being followed, and he had traffic to negotiate.

Beatrix had to capitalise on her advantage before he spotted her.

She forced the little car through the traffic, cutting between lanes to gain ground, attracting horn blares and shaken fists in her wake. Bello drove through a set of lights as they changed; she accelerated hard, jumping the red and forcing several cars and a bus to brake hard to avoid her.

The commotion was enough to make Bello notice her. He accelerated hard. Beatrix changed down and floored the accelerator. Bello swerved to avoid a truck and sideswiped a row of parked cars. The collision slowed him long enough for Beatrix to regain some of her lost ground.

Bello swung the truck into a sharp right-hand turn; Beatrix mounted the kerb and cut the corner, using fast heel-and-toe work to put the car into a controlled slide across the pavement. The truck was only a few lengths ahead now. She pushed harder until she was right behind him.

The truck's brake lights came on hard. She yanked the wheel to the left, striking the tailgate a glancing blow as she passed. She was alongside Bello now. He opened his window and pointed a pistol directly at her.

She swerved again as Bello unloaded four slugs into the Renault. The side windows exploded, and one bullet tore into the passenger headrest, ripping out jagged chunks of foam.

Beatrix jerked the wheel back to the right, and the two vehicles slammed together.

The collision caught Bello off guard, wrenching the wheel from his hand. With a roar, the truck careered across the street and crashed through the barriers of a petrol station forecourt. The impact turned the truck on its side and sent it sliding into the fuel pumps before it ground to a halt.

Beatrix fought to regain control of the Renault, but the little car slewed sideways and slammed into a steel lamp-post. The car door groaned as she forced it open and stepped gingerly out onto the pavement. Several onlookers had gathered in nervous groups and were staring and pointing in her direction.

Across the street, the pickup lay on its side, amidst the wreckage of the filling station. The horn was blaring, but there was no sign of any movement from within. Beatrix limped towards it.

As she approached, she caught the acrid odour of petrol. One of the wrecked pumps was spraying a fountain of fuel across the truck's bodywork. Beatrix used one of the truck's wheels as a foothold to pull herself up. Then she pulled at the passenger door, heaving it open far enough to look inside. The truck's engine block had been pushed back into the driving compartment, crushing the dashboard against Bello's legs and pinning him in the cabin. He strained in his seat, struggling against his seat belt and trying to grasp a pistol that lay just out of his reach.

"I'll kill you for this," he spat.

Beatrix reached into the vehicle and picked up the gun, tucking it safely into her waistband. "I don't think you're in much of a position to issue threats."

"See you in hell." Bello pulled something from his pocket: a cigarette lighter.

Beatrix hurled herself away from the top of the truck and hit the ground running. She had covered four paces when the truck ignited in an intense wash of heat.

45

I t took her an hour to get back to what remained of Gomez's flat and find Sister Magda. The nun had found a place to hide where she could watch the fire-fighters deal with the last of the blaze, and stay out of sight of whoever might have come to check on the results of the bomb.

"What happened?" Sister Magda said when she saw her.

Beatrix pointed up to the blackened windows of Gomez's apartment. "The man who did that won't ever do it again," she said.

Sister Magda didn't press. Instead, she looked around as the grey light of dawn appeared behind the apartment blocks. "What do we do now?" There was a note of desperation in her voice.

"The first thing is to get you somewhere safe," she said. "We have no way of knowing if Rincon has sent anyone else after us."

Sister Magda shook her head. "I just can't stop thinking about Julian," she said. "One minute we were talking to him, and the next... Oh, dear Lord." She closed her eyes and took a steadying breath.

"What will happen to the case?" Beatrix asked her.

"I only hope that his friends will continue his work."

Beatrix bit her lip. "I don't know if that's possible now. The evidence..."

Sister Magda's mouth fell open as realisation dawned. "Oh no."

"He had some of it with him," Beatrix said. "The rest was in the apartment in your binder. I doubt there's anything left."

The colour drained from Sister Magda's face. "Then it was all for nothing. All those people who died. Father Jair and Julian. What was the point of any of it? I've let them all down."

Beatrix shook her head. "If we can't settle this in the courts, we can do it my way instead."

Sister Magda stared at her for several seconds. "What do you mean? What are you going to do?"

"What I came here to do," said Beatrix.

"No," she said. "There has to be another way."

"Can you think of one?"

Sister Magda looked away.

"Rincon will be at Ferdinand's house tonight. It's now or never."

"You're going to kill him?"

"Both of them. They're each as guilty as the other."

Sister Magda's hand went to her mouth. "I can't stand behind that. Murder... It's never right."

"Well, you can either come up with a better idea or try to stop me. This has all gone too far. I'm not going to let him do what he's been doing any longer. The Rincons and Ferdinands of this world need to be flushed out of the gene pool."

Sister Magda looked as if she was about to protest, then stopped and looked away again. "'But if there is harm, then you shall pay life for life, eye for eye, tooth for tooth, hand for hand, foot for foot, burn for burn, wound for wound, stripe for stripe.'"

"What's that?"

"Exodus 21, verses twenty-three to twenty-five. The punishment should match the crime." She paused, looking uncomfortable. "Perhaps I have focused for too long on what my conscience has told me. Perhaps I have been wrong."

Beatrix knew a little of her Bible and knew that Jesus had suggested that the Old Testament verses should not be taken literally. But she was not minded to counter Sister Magda's conclusion; she didn't need the nun's blessing to do what she wanted to do—and what Michael had ordered her to do, come to that—but it would make things easier if she was prepared to accept that it was the only possible way forward.

Sister Magda looked up. "It will be dangerous, though?"

"It's what I'm trained for. It's the only thing I've ever been any good at."

"I will help."

"No. I don't need help, and you don't need blood on your hands. I have to get you somewhere safe."

Beatrix drove them to the convent. They had decided it was the best place for Sister Magda to hide. It wasn't ideal, but Beatrix reasoned that the police would have moved on from there by now, given the bomb blast, and Sister Magda was certain that no one there would give her away.

There were no signs of life on the street. Beatrix had driven around the block to look for suspicious cars, but there was nothing. Sister Magda was asleep in the passenger seat. Beatrix shook her gently by the shoulder.

"We're here."

The nun woke and looked around. "Are you sure this is the right thing to do?"

"It's the *only* thing. We've got no other options."

"An eye for an eye," Sister Magda said again. "I never particularly liked the Old Testament." She smoothed down her dress. "Will I see you again?"

"Probably not."

"Then I will pray for you."

Beatrix knew that no amount of prayer could absolve her of the things that she had done, but she kept that to herself. "Thank you."

"Thank *you*," Sister Magda said. "For everything."

She bowed her head and got out of the car. Beatrix watched her cross the road to the entrance and tug on the bell pull. The door was opened, there was a brief conversation, and then Sister Magda stepped inside and was gone.

46

R odrigo Ferdinand was a happy man. He watched the first of the VIP limousines roll up the gravel drive as the glitterati, the political aristocracy and the Venezuelan elite made their way to his door. He greeted them from in front of a giant ice sculpture of Simon de Bolivar that was backlit with the colours of the Venezuelan flag.

Sharp-suited waiters passed among the crowd, offering canapés and filling glasses with vintage Krug. Ferdinand shook hands with senators, gangsters, lingerie models, writers, film producers and a man in traditional robes and feathers who claimed to be a shaman and who was already half drunk. He smiled with self-satisfaction. His house was the centre of the Venezuelan social scene tonight. This was the place where anyone who was anyone would want to be seen.

The guest of honour looked less happy. Rincon wore the expression of a man waiting for root canal treatment.

"I don't know any of these people," he hissed. "How do you know they are safe?"

"Shut *up*," whispered Ferdinand through a tight smile as he prepared to greet an executive from a United States oil concern. The corporation's generous contributions to Ferdinand's charitable trust had secured him exclusive exploration contracts on tribal lands.

"I'm nervous."

"There are four armed guards patrolling outside and another four inside the house. Just relax and enjoy yourself."

"Have you forgotten what she did to Bello?"

"No, I haven't—"

"Burned him alive in his car," Rincon cut over him. "Burned him *alive!*"

"This time tomorrow you'll be safely tucked up back in your compound, and you can start making money for both of us. But, please—you need to relax. There are people coming who we'll need on our side."

"I need to go to the bathroom." Rincon gave a small, reflexive sniff.

Ferdinand rolled his eyes. "For God's sake, Aurelio," he said through gritted teeth. "Take it easy. You'll have a heart attack if you keep snorting."

They were interrupted by a barrage of flashguns outside the house. A young Colombian starlet stepped from her limousine and turned towards the cameras to wave. She had recently made a name for herself with a campaign for climate justice for indigenous groups. She had also—Ferdinand knew—just graduated from cocaine to the heroin supplied by her cartel boss boyfriend. Ferdinand might be able to use that to his advantage.

He turned to mention it to Rincon, but found that he was standing alone. Rincon was on his way to the bathroom, already reaching into his pocket for the packet of cocaine.

Ferdinand watched and wondered at what point he would be able to uncouple his own fortunes from those of his erstwhile partner. Rincon was unreliable, and, at some point, he was going to make a mistake from which it would be difficult to recover. They had been lucky so far in shutting down the priest and his campaign, but there was no guarantee that something like that would not emerge to trouble them in the future. Ferdinand knew that there would come a point when he would have to go it alone, and that, when the time came, he would have to dispose of Rincon.

He had no qualms about that. Business was business, after all.

47

Beatrix was in the kitchen behind the main hallway. She scanned the crowd through the crack between the double doors, trying to get a good look at Rincon and Ferdinand. Getting into the premises had been more difficult today than she had hoped, but, for another five hundred dollars, Ricky had secured her a uniform of black trousers and shirt. He had also furnished her with a waiter's hip pouch containing a bottle opener and a notepad. She tucked Bello's pistol into her waistband, concealing it under the folds of her shirt.

She watched the back of Ferdinand's head as he greeted his guests. There was no chance of making a move against him or Rincon now; she would have to wait until later in the evening when the alcohol had flowed a little more.

A waiter shoved through the doors with an empty plate of canapés, nearly colliding with her. He gave her a poisonous glare and hurried on into the kitchen.

Beatrix checked that the pistol was still secure beneath her shirt, then plucked a random platter from a prep station. The dish was laden with delicate-looking canapés.

"Charcoal biscotti with freshwater prawn sushi, caraway mayonnaise and Pacific salmon roe," the sous-chef instructed her. "Gluten-free but not vegan, and not suitable for anyone with nut allergies."

She took the tray out into the room. Ferdinand was shaking hands and laughing with his guests. Rincon was nowhere to be seen. Some of the guests had begun to gravitate towards the dining room, allowing her to move there and case the room. The house was well guarded. As well as the two armed guards on the service gate, she had seen at least two more patrolling the grounds. In addition to them, she had counted four more inside the house.

She wasn't as well prepared as she would have liked. The suppressed Glock 17 that she had taken from Bello had only four rounds left in its nine-round magazine, plus one in the chamber.

The ballroom had been transformed from her visit the previous day. A dozen tables glittered with cut glass and silverware, and every place setting included a small party favour box that bore the name of a famous New York jeweller. A sound system had been set up against one wall, and a lavish table on a raised platform awaited the guests of honour.

She considered the guards. They had the arrogant bearing of men who were used to getting their own way. Local heavies, perhaps, recruited more for their menace than their skill. The men patrolling outside looked like regular soldiers, probably sent as a favour by a local military commander.

She left the ballroom, still bearing her tray, and glanced up the red-carpeted staircase, which was blocked off by a velvet rope. She wanted to have a look around the rest of the house. She remembered seeing little during her previous visit to Ferdinand's study, and knew that if he had any evidence that might prove useful, it would have to be upstairs. The study had been for show; there had to be another office where he did his business.

She started towards the stairs, looking for a spot to ditch the tray, and then stopped. Rincon was pushing through the crowd towards her. He looked awful: his eyes bulged and twitched, and his forehead was beaded with sweat. He pushed straight past her without seeming to notice her and headed towards the staircase. He unhooked the velvet rope and took the stairs two at a time.

Beatrix looked around quickly. No one was paying her any attention. Setting the tray on a sideboard, she started up the stairs and reached the landing above. Two long corridors stretched away to the left and right.

There was no sign of Rincon.

She went left, carefully trying each door in turn. All of them were locked, and she could hear nothing over the sound of the music from downstairs.

She reached the end and started back towards the stairs and then stopped. A door opened at the other end of the corridor, and a man stepped into the hall. Rincon. He sniffed before taking a square of linen from his pocket and wiping his nose.

He put the handkerchief away, looked up and saw her.

Rincon froze, then pulled in a deep breath and bellowed, *"Help!"*

48

"**H**elp!" shrieked Rincon again. "Guards!"

The music downstairs was deafening now, and no one came up the stairs in response to Rincon's plea.

Beatrix moved.

Now or never.

Rincon was closer to the stairs than she was. He began to run.

He began to yell again, his voice rising in panic. "She's here! She's going to kill me!"

The guests nearest the foot of the stairs turned, looking first at each other and then craning their necks to look for the source of the shouting.

Rincon flung himself around the edge of the banister and started to run down the stairs. Beatrix pulled the pistol and took aim at the back of his head.

She squeezed off the round just as Rincon lost his footing and plunged headfirst onto the marble floor of the hallway.

Beatrix reached the top of the stairs and looked down.

Rincon's body was spread-eagled across the tiles, and a pool of blood was spreading slowly around his head.

The guests screamed. Crystal glasses shattered on the marble floor, and canapés were trodden into greasy smears as men and women scrambled for the doors. Several were elbowed aside in the rush, and an elderly woman, draped in diamonds, was knocked to the floor. There was a shout from the ballroom as two of the black-suited guards rushed into the hallway with Ferdinand close behind. Both guards had drawn their weapons. They stopped, searching for the shooter, then spied Beatrix, aimed and fired.

Beatrix was already moving. She vaulted the low balustrade and landed in the hallway so that the staircase was between her and the guards. She absorbed the impact in her legs and came up running, lurching through the kitchen's swing doors and knocking aside a waiter. Startled kitchen staff turned in her direction.

Beatrix moved to the centre of the room, keeping an eye on the double doors as she waited for the guards to follow. She didn't need to check to know that she was low on ammunition: one in the chamber and three more in the magazine.

Not nearly enough.

The door opened, and one of the guards burst through. She fired, the shot finding its mark.

Three guards left inside the house. Four more outside.

Two more men came through the doors fast and low, guns drawn, splitting right and left to duck behind the nearest counters. Beatrix went low as a volley of pistol shots spattered the wall behind her, punching penny-sized holes into the stainless-steel extraction hoods.

There was a pause, and she heard the sound of a weapon being reloaded. She stood and saw a cropped head just above the level of a counter to her right. She fired. A greasy spray of blood and bone splashed across the wall.

The second man fired a panicked shot, his bullet going high and splintering a wall tile behind Beatrix.

She squeezed off a round and then another.

She pulled the trigger again.

Nothing.

She was dry.

She hurled the weapon at the guard, then grabbed a saucepan from the gas range behind her. It was full of hot oil. She flicked her wrist and sent the oil in the direction of her assailant. The searing-hot fat splashed across his face and neck. He dropped his weapon and fell backwards, shrieking in pain. Beatrix vaulted the counter and collected the weapon that he had dropped. She put a bullet into his head, then retrieved spare magazines from both dead men and tucked them into her pockets.

The hall outside the kitchen was quiet. There was no sign of the fourth guard or any of the soldiers. It would have been a short and unpleasant battle for her if they had come all at once.

She took off the black shirt that Ricky had given her and tossed it aside. She was wearing a T-shirt beneath it and, although her lack of formal wear would stand out amidst the guests, it wouldn't be what the guards were looking for.

She went to one of the large industrial stoves and found another saucepan of fat that had been left to heat, abandoned when the staff fled from the kitchen. It bubbled and spat, already too hot. Beatrix took her lighter out of her pouch, tore off a strip of paper from a menu and lit it. She dropped the burning paper into the saucepan and stood back as the oil erupted in flame. She wrapped her hand in a dish cloth, grabbed the searing-hot handle and poured the burning oil over the hob. The flames licked greedily over the surface, sending a cloud of thick black smoke up past the fume hood to the ceiling.

She shoved the gun back in her waistband and took a knife from a nearby block. She reversed it, obscuring the blade with her arm, and slipped through the doors into the hallway. The marble floor was littered with ice, spilled drinks, squashed canapés and a solitary high-heeled shoe. Guests were still trying to shove their way out of the dining room, their escape hindered by the bottleneck at the main doors. She saw Ferdinand kneeling by Rincon's body, a guard keeping a lookout behind him. Beatrix joined the scrum and allowed herself to be nudged towards the door. She kept her eye on Ferdinand and was pleased to see the guard urge him to get up before ushering him towards the exit. She held back a little so that Ferdinand could get ahead of her, and then followed in his wake.

As she drew closer, she could see that the guard was wearing a microphone and earpiece and was conferring with colleagues somewhere in the building or grounds. Ferdinand was pale, looking back to the unmoving body of his former business partner and then to the door.

Then someone yelled, "Fire!"

One of the guests closest to a fire alarm switch on the wall smashed the protective glass panel with the heel of her shoe and activated it. The response was immediate: the alarms started to blare, and sprinklers hidden in the ceiling gushed water down onto the guests.

Ferdinand and the guard were just ahead of her now.

Beatrix reached out and grabbed the guard by the shoulder. "Look! *Look!* The kitchen's on fire!"

The man stopped and turned, his attention moving from her to the clouds of smoke that were now billowing out of the double doors. Ferdinand turned and followed the guard's gaze—and then noticed Beatrix. She didn't give him the chance to say anything. She reversed the knife, reached around Ferdinand's body and brought the blade across his throat.

He dropped to his knees, his hands clutched to his neck in a pointless attempt to try to staunch the flow of blood.

Beatrix dropped the knife and slipped between a man in a tuxedo and a woman in an evening dress. She was outside and striding away in the sunshine as she heard the guard call out for help.

But, by then, it was too late.

She was already gone.

EPILOGUE

The public address system chimed, followed by a torrent of Spanish announcing the departure of Chilean flight LATAM 475 from Tomás de Heres Airport to Santiago. Beatrix checked her boarding pass. Everything was in order. All around her, her fellow passengers began to gather their bags and shuffle towards the queue for the boarding gate.

It had been a long few days. She had escaped unnoticed from the grounds of Ferdinand's house and disappeared into the streets. She had given some thought to returning to Sister Magda at the convent, but had dismissed the idea. The nun was safer with her out of her life, especially now that all of the loose ends had been tidied up. Instead, Beatrix had headed towards the state capital, Ciudad Bolivar, a low-rise colonial town of pastel shades and palms and shady verandas. She had found a quiet hotel near the river and hunkered down in her room while she waited for a reply from Michael.

She had kept an eye on the news and had been rewarded with a small wire-service story stating that an investigation had been opened into events at the mine owned by Aurelio Rincon. It turned out that the lawyers to whom Gomez had spoken about the case had taken copies of the documents he had provided. While the file was not as voluminous as the one that had been lost in the explosion, there was enough, Beatrix read, for a prosecution to be opened. Rincon's death had robbed the locals of seeing justice delivered by way of a trial, but Beatrix doubted that they would mind that overmuch. Rincon was gone, and the prosecution would sweep up the remnants of his operation and, perhaps, deliver them a better life.

Another article the following day suggested that the government would take over operations at the mine, and that standards for the workers and their families would be guaranteed. The reporter had spoken with an unnamed 'local nun,' who said that she had been promised that the medical facilities that Rincon had destroyed would be restored as a matter of the utmost urgency. Beatrix wondered whether it would be too much to hope that Fuego and the men and women he led would be able to return from the forest and obtain treatment for their conditions.

A courier had arrived with a package for her two days after the second article had appeared. She had opened the envelope to find a new passport in the name of Mary O'Brien and a plane ticket to New Zealand, via Santiago.

There was also a handwritten note.

We'll talk when you land – M.

She turned in her seat and looked around the departure hall; it was the usual wasteland of coffee stalls, tourist shops and sleeping backpackers, and reasonably empty now. Beatrix took out her burner phone and opened a browser, navigating to the BBC website. She had bookmarked an article that she had started to read in the taxi on the way over that afternoon. She resumed reading it now, and was pleased to see that the investigation into the mine had been extended to include the involvement of Rodrigo Ferdinand, Venezuela's former minister for energy and mining. Ferdinand had been murdered during a party at his mansion, the article stated, and the police officer in charge was quoted as saying that the suspect was still at large. She was described as a white woman with blonde hair, of average height and build, and believed to be in her forties.

On her first night at the hotel, Beatrix had dyed her hair black and trimmed it into a pixie cut. Although she was a little more anxious here in the airport than she had been in the seclusion of her hotel room, she was confident that she wouldn't be stopped on her way out of the country. After all, this wasn't the first time that she had exfiltrated under these kinds of circumstances; she hoped, though, that it might be the last.

Michael had promised that, this time, he would deliver her to Isabella. She didn't trust him and never would. Beatrix knew that she provided him with a valuable service that he wouldn't be able to replace if the reason for her connection to him was removed, but she had no other choice but to go along with what he said. He maintained that he knew where Isabella was being kept and had promised that, once Beatrix had completed this job, he would reunite them. Like it or not, Michael Yeung was her best—her only—chance of finding her daughter.

Beatrix looked up at the slow-moving queue of passengers and rose to join it. The flight to New Zealand would take the better part of a day, but the journey, and everything that had led up to it, would be worth it a hundred times over if her little girl was waiting when she arrived.

GET EXCLUSIVE JOHN MILTON MATERIAL

Building a relationship with my readers is the very best thing about writing. John Milton is my best known series, and if you join my Readers' Club you'll get information on new books and deals plus all this free content:

1. A free copy of Milton's adventure in North Korea - 1000 Yards.

2. A free copy of Milton's battle with the Mafia and an assassin called Tarantula.

You can get your content **for free**, by signing up here.

ALSO BY MARK DAWSON

IN THE JOHN MILTON SERIES

The Cleaner

Sharon Warriner is a single mother in the East End of London, fearful that she's lost her young son to a life in the gangs. After John Milton saves her life, he promises to help. But the gang, and the charismatic rapper who leads it, is not about to cooperate with him.

Buy The Cleaner

Saint Death

John Milton has been off the grid for six months. He surfaces in Ciudad Juárez, Mexico, and immediately finds himself drawn into a vicious battle with the narco-gangs that control the borderlands.

Buy Saint Death

The Driver

When a girl he drives to a party goes missing, John Milton is worried. Especially when two dead bodies are discovered and the police start treating him as their prime suspect.

<u>Buy The Driver</u>

Ghosts

John Milton is blackmailed into finding his predecessor as Number One. But she's a ghost, too, and just as dangerous as him. He finds himself in deep trouble, playing the Russians against the British in a desperate attempt to save the life of his oldest friend.

<u>Buy Ghosts</u>

The Sword of God

On the run from his own demons, John Milton treks through the Michigan wilderness into the town of Truth. He's not looking for trouble, but trouble's looking for him. He finds himself up against a small-town cop who has no idea with whom he is dealing, and no idea how dangerous he is.

<u>Buy The Sword of God</u>

Salvation Row

Milton finds himself in New Orleans, returning a favour that saved his life during Katrina. When a lethal adversary from his past takes an interest in his business, there's going to be hell to pay.

Buy Salvation Row

Headhunters

Milton barely escaped from Avi Bachman with his life. But when the Mossad's most dangerous renegade agent breaks out of a maximum security prison, their second fight will be to the finish.

Buy Headhunters

The Ninth Step

Milton's attempted good deed becomes a quest to unveil corruption at the highest levels of government and murder at the dark heart of the criminal underworld. Milton is pulled back into the game, and that's going to have serious consequences for everyone who crosses his path.

Buy The Ninth Step

The Jungle

John Milton is no stranger to the world's seedy underbelly. But when the former British Secret Service agent comes up against a ruthless human trafficking ring, he'll have to fight harder than ever to conquer the evil in his path.

Buy The Jungle

Blackout

A message from Milton's past leads him to Manila and a

confrontation with an adversary he thought he would never meet again. Milton finds himself accused of murder and imprisoned inside a brutal Filipino jail - can he escape, uncover the truth and gain vengeance for his friend?

Buy Blackout

The Alamo

A young boy witnesses a murder in a New York subway restroom. Milton finds him, and protects him from corrupt cops and the ruthless boss of a local gang.

Buy The Alamo

Redeemer

Milton is in Brazil, helping out an old friend with a close protection business. When a young girl is kidnapped, he finds himself battling a local crime lord to get her back.

Buy Redeemer

Sleepers

A sleepy English town. A murdered Russian spy. Milton and Michael Pope find themselves chasing the assassins to Moscow.

Buy Sleepers

Twelve Days

Milton checks back in with Elijah Warriner, but finds himself caught up in a fight to save him from a jealous - and dangerous - former friend.

Buy Twelve Days

Bright Lights

All Milton wants to do is take his classic GTO on a coast-to-coast road trip. But he can't ignore the woman on the side of the road in need of help. The decision to get involved leads to a tussle with a murderous cartel that he thought he had put behind him.

Buy Bright Lights

The Man Who Never Was

John Milton is used to operating in the shadows, weaving his way through dangerous places behind a fake identity. Now, to avenge the death of a close friend, he must wear his mask of deception once more.

Buy The Man Who Never Was

Killa City

John Milton has a nose for trouble. He can smell it a mile away. And when he witnesses a suspicious altercation between a young man and two thugs in a car auction parking lot, he can't resist getting involved.

Buy Killa City

Ronin

Milton travels to Bali in search of a new identity. He meets a young woman who has been forced to work for the Yakuza in Japan, and finds himself drawn into danger in an attempt to keep her safe.

Buy Ronin

Never Let Me Down Again

A human rights activist has vanished without a trace and his dying mother is desperate to know the truth. When the mysterious disappearance leads Milton all the way to the Western Isles of Scotland, he sees an opportunity to find an old friend and finally make amends for a mistake that cost him dearly. Milton is determined to track both men down, wherever his search may lead.

Buy Never Let Me Down Again

Bulletproof

Captured and imprisoned by the organisation he once worked for, Milton must do one last job in exchange for his freedom. Bullheaded billionaire fixer Tristan Huxley is brokering a weapons deal between Russia and India. He needs protection and he wants Milton by his side. Huxley has trusted Milton with his life before but these days his world is more decadent and his enemies more dangerous, in ways that nobody could ever have suspected.

Buy Bulletproof

Uppercut

John Milton is on the run again. Chasing clues to help him understand the new risks he faces, he finds himself in

Dublin. Before he knows it, he is involved with a woman who has fallen foul of a dangerous local family. Out in 2023.

Buy Uppercut

IN THE BEATRIX ROSE SERIES

In Cold Blood

Beatrix Rose was the most dangerous assassin in an off-the-books government kill squad until her former boss betrayed her. A decade later, she emerges from the Hong Kong underworld with payback on her mind. They gunned down her husband and kidnapped her daughter, and now the debt needs to be repaid. It's a blood feud she didn't start but she is going to finish.

Buy In Cold Blood

Blood Moon Rising

There were six names on Beatrix's Death List and now there are four. She's going to account for the others, one by one, even if it kills her. She has returned from Somalia with another target in her sights. Bryan Duffy is in Iraq, surrounded by mercenaries, with no easy way to get to him and no easy way to get out. And Beatrix has other issues that need to be addressed. Will Duffy prove to be one kill too far?

Buy Blood Moon Rising

Blood and Roses

Beatrix Rose has worked her way through her Kill List. Four are dead, just two are left. But now her foes know she has them in her sights and the hunter has become the hunted.

Buy Blood and Roses

The Dragon and the Ghost

Beatrix Rose flees to Hong Kong after the murder of her husband and the kidnapping of her child. She needs money. The local triads have it. What could possibly go wrong?

Buy The Dragon and the Ghost

Tempest

Two people adrift in a foreign land, Beatrix Rose and Danny Nakamura need all the help they can get. A storm is coming. Can they help each other survive it and find their children before time runs out for both of them?

Buy Tempest

Phoenix

She does Britain's dirty work, but this time she needs help.
Beatrix Rose, meet John Milton...

<u>Buy Phoenix</u>

IN THE ISABELLA ROSE SERIES

The Angel

Isabella Rose is recruited by British intelligence after a terrorist attack on Westminster.

<u>Buy The Angel</u>

The Asset

Isabella Rose, the Angel, is used to surprises, but being abducted is an unwelcome novelty. She's relying on Michael Pope, the head of the top-secret Group Fifteen, to get her back.

<u>Buy The Asset</u>

The Agent

Isabella Rose is on the run, hunted by the very people she had been hired to work for. Trained killer Isabella and former handler Michael Pope are forced into hiding in India and, when a mysterious informer passes them clues on the whereabouts of Pope's family, the prey see an opportunity to become the predators.

Buy The Agent

The Assassin

Ciudad Juárez, Mexico, is the most dangerous city in the world. And when a mission to break the local cartel's grip goes wrong, Isabella Rose, the Angel, finds herself on the wrong side of prison bars. Fearing the worst, Isabella plays her only remaining card...

Buy The Assassin

The Avenger

Living under new identities in rural France, Isabella Rose and Michael Pope are trying to lay low. Tired of hiding, all Isabella wants is the chance to live an ordinary life. But Isabella is an extraordinary young woman and the people pursuing her will never, ever, give up. Her unique abilities have attracted the attention of the Academy of Military Science in Beijing. And it's not only Isabella who needs to stay in the shadows. Pope has his fair share of enemies and a family that he's desperate to protect.

Buy The Avenger

IN THE ATTICUS PRIEST SERIES

The House in the Woods

Disgraced detective Atticus Priest investigates the murder of a family on Christmas Eve. He's been employed to demolish the police case against his client, but things get complicated when the officer responsible for the case is his former girlfriend.

<u>Buy The House in the Woods</u>

A Place to Bury Strangers

A dog walker finds a human bone on lonely Salisbury Plain. DCI Mackenzie Jones investigates the grisly discovery but cannot explain how it ended up there. She contacts Atticus Priest and the two of them trace the bone to a graveyard in the nearby village of Imber. But the village was abandoned after it was purchased by the Ministry of Defence to train the army, so why have bodies been buried in the graveyard since the church was closed?

<u>Buy A Place to Bury Strangers</u>

ABOUT MARK DAWSON

Mark Dawson is the author of the John Milton, Beatrix and Isabella Rose and Atticus Priest series.

For more information:
www.markjdawson.com
mark@markjdawson.com

Printed in Great Britain
by Amazon

24914159R00148